TO MEND THE BROKEN-HEARTED

THE HEALER AND THE HERMIT

JUDE KNIGHT

TITCHFIELD PRESS

DEDICATION

To all the broken who think themselves unworthy of love. If someone who genuinely loves you sees the good in you, trust that love, become that good. We human beings are made to put ourselves back together, but not on our own.

We are all broken. That's how the light gets in.

(For the origin of this quote, variously ascribed, see https://quoteinvestigator.-com/2016/11/16/light/)

AUTHOR'S NOTE

My fictional family comes from an entirely imaginary kingdom hidden high in the mountains on the northeast border between Iran and Turkmenistan. Such kingdoms, called *khanates* or *kaganates*, proliferated in the troubled times as one dynasty of Iranian rulers faded and another had not yet come to power.

The Winderfields and their retainers are from different source countries and speak a dialect made from a mix of languages, mostly Farsi, English, and Turkmen. If a term is important, I'll usually explain it when it is first used.

From ancient times, westerners called Iran '*Persia*' after the great empire Alexander the Great conquered more than 2000 years ago, and my hero occasionally uses that term when talking to the English. To those living in Iran, Persia was just one ancient kingdom in what was originally called *Eran-shahr* or *Airan-shahr*, which means 'the place of the Aryans'. This evolved to become Iran-shahr and, by the time of my story, just Iran.

TO MEND THE BROKEN-HEARTED

Ruth Winderfield is miserable in London's ballrooms, where her family's wealth and questions over her birth make her a target for the unscrupulous and a pariah to the high-sticklers. Trained as a healer, she is happiest in a sickroom. When a smallpox epidemic traps her at the remote manor of a reclusive lord, the last thing she expects is to find her heart's desire.

Valentine, Earl of Ashbury, was carried home from war three years ago, unconscious, a broken man. He woke to find his family in ruins, his faithless wife and treacherous brother dead, his family's two girl children exiled to school. He becomes a near recluse while he spends his days trying to restore the estate, or at least prevent further crumbling.

When an impertinent, bossy female turns up with several sick children, including the two girls, he reluctantly gives them shelter. Unable to stand by and watch the suffering, he begins to help with the nursing, while he falls irrevocably for both girls and the lovely Ruth.

The epidemic over, Ruth and Val part ways, each reluctant to share how they feel without a sign from the other. Ruth returns to her family and the ton. Val begins to build a new life centred on his girls. But danger to Ruth is a clarion call Val cannot ignore. If they can stop the villains determined to destroy them, perhaps the hermit and the healer can mend one another's hearts.

1

shbury Hall, Leicestershire, April 1813

The crows rose in a flock over the tower, a cacophony on wings. Val straightened and shaded his eyes, peering to see if he could tell what had spooked them. It was unlikely to be a traveller. After three years of repulsing visitors, he had none, and few people used the lane that branched towards the manor from the road that passed the tower. The only people he ever saw were his tenant farmers and the few servants who kept the crumbling monstrosity he lived in marginally fit for human habitation.

He set the team moving, the plough and seed drill combination creating a row of furrows behind him, but called a halt again when a bird shot up from almost under the horses' hooves. Sure enough, a lapwing nest lay right in the path of the plough. Val carefully steered around it. He knew his concern for the pretty things set his tenants laughing behind his back, but the birds didn't take up much room, and they'd soon hatch their chicks and be off to better cover.

One more evidence of his madness, the tenants thought, and in his worst moments he thought they were right, when thunder set him shaking, or nightmares woke him screaming defiance, or approaching anywhere close to that cursed tower froze him in his tracks.

The clouds that had threatened to disgorge all day finally sent a few stray drops his way, portents of more to come. However, another half-hour would see the spring corn planted at last. He had a bare two passes more to finish, and Barrow and his son were behind him with hoes, covering in the seed.

It remained to be seen what kind of crop they'd get when the weather had delayed them a good three weeks.

The gig from the inn went by beyond the hedge that bordered the lane. What was so important that it couldn't wait until the housekeeper made her weekly trip to the nearest village? No matter. If he was needed, his manservant knew where to find him. He guided the team into the tight turn that would begin the second-to-last pass.

The rain thickened by the time he turned into the last row, and soaked into the ground enough to make heavy going before he was halfway down the field. The ingenious device on the end of his crippled arm allowed him to manage a well-trained team, but they were now tired and the extra effort made them restive.

"Just a bit more," he coaxed the horses, "just a bit more."

The estate blacksmith had made several hand-replacing devices, each with its own use, and the carpenter had carved a reasonable facsimile of his lost appendage for social occasions. Not that he'd worn it. Pinning the sleeve shut at the end of his stump was good enough when he didn't require the blacksmith's mechanisms.

The inn's gig passed back along the lane in the direction of the village of Ashhurst. Had it been making a delivery? His housekeeper had not mentioned any lack. His mind on the ploughing, he'd almost forgotten the gig by the time they at last reached the end.

"That's it done, then, milord," Barrow said, wiping his face. It was as wet again a moment later.

Val agreed, habituation allowing him to hide his wince at being addressed with his brother's title. Three years had not been enough to stop his reaction, but at least no one needed to know. "Get these boys home and give them a good feed," he said, giving the lead horse a firm pat with his true hand. "They've done well, and just in time."

"That I will, milord. And you get yourself indoors, sir. Thankee," Barrow said.

Did the man think Val too stupid or too far gone to go inside out of the rain? Well. No point in staying wet just to prove he was his own master. Val left Barrow to his son and horses, and set off to trudge back through the fields to the house, running the last few hundred yards through blinding hail.

Crick, his manservant, fussed over his towel and his bath and his dry clothes, and Val allowed it. This kind of weather was too much like Albuera for Crick's demons, immersing him back into the confusion and the pain. Val told himself that he kept the old soldier out of compassion. During his worst moments, he feared his motivation was more a sick desire to have someone around who was even less sane than he was.

By the time Val was warm and dry again, the thunder had started. He sent Crick off to bed. There'd be no more sense out of the poor man tonight, nor much from Val, either. He refused the offer of dinner and shut himself up in his room so no one would see him whimpering in his sleep as the rumblings overhead fuelled his nightmares.

It was not until the following day, after the thunderstorm had passed, that he remembered the gig. Mrs Minnich, who was house-keeper and cook, remembered that it had delivered mail, and thought Crick had taken it, but what happened after that no one knew, least of all Crick. He had got roaring drunk and surfaced late in the day with a bad headache, a worse conscience, and no memory of the previous day at all.

The inn might know who the letter was from; even what it was about, since they'd sent someone out with it despite the weather. Minnich took a note to them on Friday, her regular day for shop-ping. She came back with the message that the gig had brought several letters, one of them marked urgent. It was from the school to which his sister-in-law had exiled the girls before she absconded with the contents of the jewel safe shortly after she was made a widow, before Val even knew his brother's death had made him the earl.

The situation wasn't the girls' fault, but he still didn't want to see either of them. He put the girls out of his head with the ease of long practice, along with any curiosity about the message. There were fields to plough, repairs to be made, and animal breeding to plan. If what the school wanted was important, no doubt they would write again.

Leicestershire, May 1813

It had been raining for the last half-hour, and the girls huddling on top of the coach must be miserable. They were safer up there with her bodyguard and friend, Zyba, and Albert, the coachman, than inside the darkened coach where their two sick schoolmates and the maid from the school burned with fever, coughed helplessly, and begged for water.

Surely this nightmare trip must soon be over? They had made camp each night rather than expose an inn full of innocent people to the illness. More, they had kept to two parties. Zyba and the coachman, who had already had ābele—smallpox, as these English called it—remained with those who had been staying at the school.

Zyba had been her dearest friend since they were children at their mothers' knees. She had protested staying apart from Ruth, leaving Ruth to bear the burden of nursing. But someone Ruth trusted had to look after the other girls.

Ruth's mounted escort kept apart: far enough away to remain well but close enough to provide protection. Not that Ruth expected such a well-armed party to be attacked, but her father had insisted on extra caution sins their cousin attempted to kill them last year.

The coach turned. Ruth looked away from her patients for long enough to peer out the window. "The old stone watchtower marks the border of Ashbury land," they had been told at the nearby village. "Turn at the tower and continue on the main lane until you come to the carriageway to the manor."

Jeyhun, head of the horsemen, had reported that the stable master at the inn seemed startled at their destination. "Earl of Ashbury don't have many visitors," he'd said. Ashbury would have to have some now. If little Lady Genevieve were the only one ill, Ruth would still be reluctant to leave her to the care of unknown servants. She certainly did not intend for her other two patients to travel on, and she would not expect this Lord Ashbury to take responsibility for them beyond giving them shelter.

They lurched along the rutted, overgrown lane for another mile, possibly more. Either it had been a harsh winter or Lord Ashbury did little maintenance. Eventually, as promised, the lane terminated in the forecourt of a large manor, and the carriage pulled up at a sweep of steps, once grand but now crumbling, with weeds growing in the cracks.

By the time Ruth opened the door to get a better view through the streaming rain, Zyba had leapt down from the roof. "I will take the girls inside, *şazada gyz*, and then return for these." She flicked a hand at the interior of the carriage behind her.

"Bring blankets to keep off the worst of the rain," Ruth suggested. A sudden squall blew the rain straight into her face and she withdrew into the carriage and closed the door, but continued to watch as Zyba climbed the steps to bang on the door of the manor house as Albert helped the girls to clamber down from the carriage.

All three girls had joined Zyba by the time the door opened a few inches. The guard leaned forward to speak, then, in a sudden move, thrust her boot into the closing gap and threw her shoulder against the door. It crashed open, but Zyba didn't follow it, instead calling out in the polyglot tongue of Pari Daisa, Ruth's birthplace, "Jeyhun, secure this hall. Don't hurt the inhabitants, but make sure our lady can bring her patients in out of the rain."

Jeyhun had been holding his men off to one side, still mounted. At Zyba's call, he led two of them up the stairs, leaving one to hold the horses and one to take station by the carriage, though who he imagined was going to attack them on the forecourt of an English manor, Ruth could not imagine.

Before he reached the door, however, Lord Ashbury's daughter ducked under Zyba's restraining arm and entered the hall, shouting, "Mrs Minnich! It's me. Mirrie. I've come home."

Zyba and Jeyhun followed Lady Mirabelle, and a moment later Zyba popped her head out the door again, grinned and nodded at Ruth, and beckoned the other girls inside, closing the door.

Ruth waited with what patience she could muster, occupying her time by checking each of her patients. Lady Genevieve was far too hot, though she shivered as if with cold. Were it not for the rain, Ruth would have both doors open to cool the air, for this close atmosphere could not be helping. The other girl, Anne Bush, was also in the fever stage, wracked with coughs, no pustules as yet. She sat huddled in her nest of blankets, her wide eyes watching Ruth's every move. The servant, Jeffries, was coughing helplessly in her corner, but still insisting, "I'm fine, milady."

At last, Zyba was there again, with two men Ruth didn't know. "These are the men who know that they've had the disease, princess," Zyba said in the Pari Daisa dialect. One of the men lifted Jeffries, and the other took up Lady Genevieve. Zyba held out her arms for Anne.

Ruth refused. "Stand well back," she warned, as she climbed from the carriage and reached into it for the child. A maid waited with an umbrella, but Ruth waved her away and hurried up the short flight of stairs.

Another maid just inside the door held a candelabra against the gloom that prevailed inside the house. Zyba kept talking as she followed Ruth up the steps and into the house. "They are setting up rooms for us in an unused wing. Much of the house is abandoned, it seems, but that is all to the good for a quarantine. I have ordered our baggage brought as soon as it can be, also bathing water and food."

Food. Ruth had not allowed herself to realise how hungry she was. How tired, too. Her knees almost buckled as exhaustion rushed in on her at the prospect of a wash, a meal, and a bed within four walls. She pushed it back. She had days of round-the-clock nursing ahead of her; weeks, perhaps, if the disease spread.

They traversed a long narrow hall, shabby and sparsely furnished but clean, and went through a door into another hall at right-angles. This one had all the signs of a hasty and incomplete cleaning—every horizontal surface above floor level was thick with dust, cobwebs still hung in tatters from the picture rails, streaks of mud showed where a wet mop had been pushed along the dusty floor, and elongated dust balls shifted restlessly against the wainscoting as they passed.

They turned a corner. The maid with the candelabra opened a door and led them into a room where two more maids worked under the supervision of a short woman neatly dressed in a subdued gown of a considerably superior cut and fabric to those worn by the maids.

She turned at their entrance and hurried towards them, stopping to lay her palm against Lady Genevieve's forehead. "She is so hot, the poor little angel, but I would have known her anywhere." She caught Ruth's gaze on her, and flushed, stepping away to wave the footman carrying Lady Genevieve to the freshly made bed in one corner before addressing Zyba directly.

"This chamber is for Lady Genevieve. I know you said to put four beds in here, Miss, but it cannot be right to have these other people in the same room. Lady Genevieve is his lordship's niece!"

Ruth was too tired to tolerate the very English outrage over a perceived breach of the social order. "Lady Zyba obeyed my orders, Mrs…?"

The woman answered the unspoken question, her agitated hands twisting her apron. "Minnich, Miss. I am the housekeeper here."

Zyba, her face stern, corrected Mrs Minnich. "The correct English form of address is 'my lady'. In her father's kingdom, it would be 'your highness' or 'excellency'. Lady Ruth is a doctor, and you will obey her in all things, as do I, so that your young mistress might live."

That little speech hit all the right notes; Mrs Minnich bowed to superior status and her concern for the child, though her eyes showed alarm at the concept of a female doctor. "I will have more beds fetched, my lady," she agreed. "I am sorry we were not ready… I did not know you were coming, my lady."

Ruth did not like that Lady Genevieve showed no interest in the fact she was home. She lay listless on the bed, moving only to cough. "We must have those beds immediately so I can make my patients comfortable. My people will help yours." She put Anne down on the other end of Lady Genevieve's bed, and touched the arm of the footman burdened with Jeffries, pointing to a chair with a deep seat and a footstool before it. "This chair looks comfortable." Also dirty,

but it could not be helped. The man settled Jeffries in it, and spread
a blanket over her without being asked.

"Now, Minnich, I need those beds." She fixed the housekeeper
with a stern look. "I need this room as clean as your maids can
make it without raising dust and noise to hurt my patients. Also,
warm water for washing and our baggage from the coach. And
something for my patients to drink—lemonade, if you have it."

The housekeeper sprang into action with an efficiency that
belied the near-terminal neglect all around Ruth in this wing of the
house. Ruth bent to the task of getting her patients to drink, while
all around her the room was transformed.

2

—————

Val heard Crick before he saw him. "My lord, my lord," the man was shouting, his voice high with barely suppressed panic. Val excused himself from a discussion about clearing a blockage in a stream that was threatening to flood the young barley, and took a few paces to meet Crick as the butler came hurtling across the field, careless of the new shoots.

"My lord, we're under attack. They've captured the house, my lord."

Val took the man's arm and led him to the side of the field. "Take a deep breath, Crick," he soothed. "All is well. We are in England. For us, the war is over."

Crick pulled his arm free and so far forgot himself as to seize Val's shoulders. "No, sir, you don't understand. Soldiers on horseback. A lady with a sword. Another lady in the carriage. I tried to stop them, sir, but they forced their way into the house. They made Mrs Minnich take them to the family wing. We have to marshal the tenants, my lord, and rescue the servants."

Being addressed as 'my lord' gave Val pause. Usually, when Crick had one of his episodes, he reverted to Val's former rank. Always, in fact. When Crick called Val 'major', the whole household knew to hide anything that could be used as a weapon.

Barrow and his gangly young son had followed and were listening. Val met Barrow's concerned eyes. "A carriage and a troop of horsemen went down the lane a while back," Barrow disclosed. The lane was out of sight from here, but Barrow explained his knowledge by fetching his son a clip across the ear. "The boy here saw them when he went to fetch the axe, but didn't say nothin'."

Young Barrow's observation suggested some truth to Crick's fantasy, but it couldn't possibly be the invasion Crick imagined. What would be the point? "I'll investigate," Val decided.

Crick and Barrow protested him going alone. "Five men, my lord," Crick insisted. "Foreigners, they were, and the lady, too."

Val's troops were a half-mad butler, plus a burly tenant farmer, and his fifteen-year-old son. Val would do better alone. "You shall be my reserves," he told them. "Stay at the edge of the woods where you can see the house. If I don't come out within thirty minutes and signal that everything is safe, ride to the village for help."

Crick argued, but Val was adamant. Still, as he crossed the open ground to the house, his skin prickled with the old familiar sense of walking into enemy territory.

He diverted his path to pass the stables. Sure enough, a strange carriage stood outside the carriage house, and through the open door of the stable block he could see two strangers, one with a fork of hay and one with a bucket, heading towards the stalls. They stopped when they saw him, and stood waiting for him to approach.

Val realised why Crick had identified them as foreign. The beards would have been enough, and the skin—a copper brown that in England only field workers ever attained. The clothes confirmed it—the red tunics that flowed to mid-thigh, the loose black trousers gathered into knee high boots, the bushy sheepskin hats. They did not put down their burdens, which argued for peaceful intentions, but the weapons in their belts, their alert stance, and their wary eyes suggested that 'warrior' was the correct identification.

"Who told you to make free with my stables?" he demanded.

The man with the hay fork used his head to indicate Val's elderly stable master, who appeared from the aisle the men had been heading towards. Greggs and an equally decrepit groom managed what was left of Val's cattle.

"Is it a mistake, my lord?" Greggs stammered. "Only, Mrs Minnich said I was to let them have what they needed." His eyes lit and he smiled blissfully. "Such horses, my lord! I have never seen such horses in my stables. No, not in all my years."

The man with the hay fork bowed. "Lord Ashbury, I take it. I regret the necessity to trespass on your hospitality, your lordship." The English was near perfect, and Val could not place the slight accent any more than he could the clothing.

"You have the advantage of me," he pointed out.

The thick brows drew together over the eagle's beak of a nose. "The advantage, sir?" He cast a glance at his companion, who did not quite shrug.

"You are…?" Val prompted, and the man's face cleared.

He bowed again. "Jeyhun Rasit-ogly, sir. I have the honour to be *sederke*—you would say commander—of the escort to Lady Ruth Winderfield, daughter of the Duke of Winshire." He spoke in some foreign tongue to his companion, who bowed to Val and continued on past the stable master into the wing of the stable that still had intact stalls.

"I have told him to continue watering the horses," Rasit-ogly explained. "May I be of further service, Lord Ashbury?"

Val opened his mouth to ask further questions, then closed it again. Better to speak to this duke's daughter directly. He shook his head and Rasit-ogly bowed again and went after his companion.

Val crossed the stable yard and entered the house by the side door. He supposed he could not follow his first impulse, which was to find the aristocratic bitch who had descended on him unannounced and hurl her out to face the storm and the approaching night. She'd not treat his house like an inn for more than the one night, though. In the morning, she and her guard would be on their way.

He shrugged out of his coat and hung it on a peg to drip, shaking his head to disperse the worst of the wet. Now. Where would Mrs Minnich have deposited a duke's daughter? One of the formal parlours, he supposed. He had taken three steps along the passage to the front part of the house when a movement caught at the corner of his eye and he turned to see his housekeeper entering the kitchen, bustling with more purpose than he'd seen in an age.

"Minnich," he called.

She jumped and spun around, then waited for him to approach. "Minnich, we have a visitor, I am told."

"Indeed, my lord." She beamed. "Isn't it exciting? Your own little girl home at last. Such a pity about your niece. But there. Lady Ruth says she will stay and nurse the poor little mite, and the other two, and she is a doctor, my lord, if you've ever heard of such a thing. She seems to know what she is doing, young as she is. But there. She comes from foreign parts, and I daresay things are different there."

Reeling at the news that his wife's daughters were once again under his roof, Val couldn't summon the words to question the servant, but there was no need, as Minnich kept talking. "We're to take trays to them, and no one is to go into the old family wing. That's what Lady Ruth says.

"And those as cleaned the sickroom, we have to wash well and boil all our clothes. I'll just be ordering the trays for the sickroom, then, sir, shall I, and for the other members of her ladyship's party? Then I'll be off to me bath?"

Val nodded, allowing her to escape. The family wing? He had locked it after the… after everything had gone wrong, and no one had been in it since. Not that he'd been able to lock in the memories, but he could keep them suppressed, for the most part, as long as he stayed clear of reminders. He began to perspire at the mere thought of crossing the threshold, of returning to those rooms.

He set his jaw and strode along the narrow servant's hall that led to the wing's entrance. The duke's daughter owed him some answers.

Two of his four remaining footmen were busy cleaning in the formerly abandoned wing, supervised by a woman. He stopped just inside the door, examining her—black hair rolled into a sensible coil at the back of her head, dark eyes under firmly marked brows, slender form neatly outlined in a smart carriage dress. The rifle slung across her back and the knife in a sheath at her waist should have looked incongruous—did look incongruous. The confidence in her stance and her expression suggested she would use them at need, and use them well.

Young, Minnich had said, though Minnich probably thought of Val as young, and he would not see thirty again. The woman was early twenties, from the look. With the brown tones of her skin and the strong nose, she looked like no duke's daughter he had ever seen. Perhaps the duke in question was Spanish or Italian, with a strong mixture of Moorish blood? Further east than that, he thought, given the exotic costumes of her retainers.

"Lady Ruth?" he asked.

"This wing is in quarantine," the woman replied, her English clear and precise, with no trace of foreign intonation. "If you have a message for Lady Ruth, I will give it to her when she emerges. My lady has given orders that none are to enter the sickroom."

Val seized on the last point. "Ah, yes. I am told my   ah   niece is ill. What of my…" he could not bring himself to call the girl his daughter, though, in all truth, she might be. "What of Lady Mirabelle?"

The unnamed lady tipped her head to one side as she examined him. "You are the earl, then. Your daughter is well, as yet, but all who have been in contact with the patients are in quarantine. Do you wish to speak with her?"

He shook his head, suppressing a wince. "Not at the moment." He would have to face the child at some point, he supposed, but not unprepared. He had to have his emotions under control so he did not upset her. He wasn't so far lost to sense that he wanted to punish the child for the sins of the adults. It wasn't her fault that he could not bear to look at her.

"What was your mistress thinking, bringing them here?" he demanded. "They should be at the school, not racketing across the country when one of them is sick and the other subject to her contagion." He added, as an afterthought, "What is this illness?"

The foreign lady frowned. "You did not receive the letter from the school? The housekeeper seemed unaware but I thought… The school has been closed, Lord Ashbury. Smallpox. My lady was unable to leave the three girls for whom she is responsible at the school, so when you did not send instructions for your own charges, she agreed to bring them to you on her way south."

Smallpox. Val had seen it go through villages and armies, killing every third soul and leaving as many others scarred for life. It was particularly deadly for children. He'd had it himself, as a boy, and been lucky to escape with few marks.

Something of his horror must have shown, for the foreign lady assured him, "Lady Ruth has experience with such cases, my lord. She will save those who can be saved."

She put up a hand to stop the footman who was trying to sidle past. "*All* the corners, I said. This passage must be clean enough we could serve dinner from the floor."

The footman turned to Val in protest, and the woman forestalled him. "Lord Ashbury, we have found that cleanliness prevents spread of the illness. I am creating a—a firebreak, if you will —to help us maintain the quarantine."

Val had never heard of such a thing, but he had reason to know that the injured grew ill in dirty, crowded conditions. "Do as the lady says, Paul," he told the footman.

The arrival of maids with trays brought a temporary halt to Val's attempts to storm the citadel this duke's daughter and her entourage had made of his east wing. The curtseys in his direction were cursory; those to the lady deeper. "Lady Zyba, where would you like these, dear?"

Lady Zyba, was it? The name was as foreign as her appearance, for all the perfect English. She was pointing to the narrow tables along the passage. "Here, please. Lord Ashbury, we shall serve ourselves from here, to reduce the risk to your servants." The tables had held vases and ornaments when Val had last seen them, but now they were denuded, and Lady Zyba retreated beyond the furthest table so the maids could put down their burdens without passing her.

The interruption gave Val time to reorder his thoughts. When the maids retreated, followed by the footmen who had finally cleaned the passage to Lady Zyba's satisfaction, he addressed the lady again, "Lady Zyba, I will leave you, also. There shall be a footman in the hall outside this door. Let him know about anything you need. My house is at your service and that of your mistress."

What else could he do? Smallpox! He hoped this Lady Ruth was as good as her minions believed. For all his reluctance to face the two girls abandoned and bereaved by the mess he, his brother and their respective wives had made of their lives, they were his to protect. He wanted them to live.

His mind made up, he sent a messenger out into the fields to retrieve Crick and reassure the tenants.

A knock at the door attracted Ruth from her watch over her patients. "I have your dinner," Zyba said, as she stood in the doorway to the sickroom, a laden tray in her hands.

"You cannot come in, Zyba," Ruth warned.

"You will need my help," her friend insisted. "You cannot nurse all three at once, and the help we hoped for is not available here."

Ruth shook her head. "I need someone I trust to look after the other girls, and to watch them for signs of the illness." The coachman had also had smallpox, but a man could not be left in charge of young females. In England as in Pari Daisa, the thought was unconscionable. "Surely the lord here will be able to find a capable female who has had the smallpox and is young enough to assist me? If not at the manor, perhaps in one of the tenant farms or in the village?"

"I met our host," Zyba commented. "He came to say that his house will serve us. I shall ask him to speak with you, so you can tell him what you require. Eat first, dost Ruth." She put the dinner tray down just inside the doorway and stepped back.

Ruth put up a hand to stop her. "What of the other girls?"

"Well enough, for the moment. The Minnich female has put us in the old nursery, and Lady Mirabelle is discovering old friends in the toys and books." Zyba's brow furrowed for a moment. "She was excited to see Mrs Minnich, and keeps begging to visit with Lady Genevieve, but she has not asked for her father. I asked if he wished to speak with her, and he said, 'not at the moment'." Zyba shrugged. "The English are hard to fathom."

Ruth shrugged. The man was barely a father at all. The girls were aged eight years and six years, and had not left the school or had a visitor in three years, from what she understood. "Let him know I will meet with him in one hour. I will come out into the hallway if he has not had smallpox. If he has, he can come as far as this doorway."

Ruth ate her own dinner in snatched mouthfuls between feeding a little broth to Jeffries and Genevieve and dribbling water in Anne's mouth. Little and often. Some medical treatises suggested limiting fluids to manage the nausea; others proposed bleeding to lower the humours. Ruth's own teachers had declared that providing sufficient fluids to replace those lost was essential to keep the patient alive.

Sleep. Fluid. Food if they would take it. Warmth when they were chilled. Cooling by air, water or ice when they were over-heated. Soothing herbs in teas for the fever and the pain. Then, once the pustules appeared, more herbs in unguents and baths for the skin. These were all in Ruth's arsenal, to be expended in the battle for her patients' lives. She would fight to the last breath. The victory would fall where it would.

Ashbury presented himself in precisely one hour. Ruth looked around at the sound of a clearing throat and found him standing in the doorway.

"Lady Ruth Winderfield, I presume?" he asked.

Ruth looked him over, taking a moment to adjust her expectations to the reality. She had envisaged another pallid English lord, plump from overindulging at table and decanter, an arrogant belief in his own innate superiority clear in his face, his voice and the way he carried his body.

Ashbury—the accent marked him as an aristocrat when nothing else did—was a tall, lean man casually dressed in a loose coat with a coloured kerchief knotted at the throat. His face was also lean. Dark eyes alive with interest watched her from a face engraved by grief or pain. A long, jagged scar skirted the corner of his eye and bisected his cheek and then one side of his mouth, trailing to nothing on his chin. Far from being fashionably pale in the English way, this man had skin browned by the weather. One arm dangled at his side, the sleeve pinned over his wrist in place of a missing hand.

"You must be Lord Ashbury. Thank you for your hospitality, my lord. I am sorry to have brought this trouble to your house."

"I understand that you had no choice, Lady Ruth. The school has been closed, and you were kind enough to bring my—uh—the girls—uh—Mirabelle and Genevieve to their home. I do not imagine they were sick when you set out, and of course you could not abandon them. How is Genevieve?"

"She still has the fever, but the rash has begun in the mouth. We can expect the fever to decline in the next few days. The crisis will come after it rises again. None of them showed symptoms when I left the school, Lord Ashbury, but I thought it likely that one or more carried the contagion. I could not, in all conscience, leave them to be quarantined in a sick house with attendants whose response to the illness is to bleed them and purge them."

Ashbury pursed his lips and she waited for him to lecture her on her presumption, but he surprised her with a question. "Minnich tells me you are a physician. Where did you train, Lady Ruth? In the same place you acquired your warlike attendants? Somewhere in the East, I assume?"

She inclined her head in agreement. "I apprenticed with several healers, including physicians who trained at the teaching hospitals in Tehran and Baghdad. I have also studied with Western physicians, though not since my family arrived in England." She sighed. "I am well qualified to attend your niece, my lord, even though I am a woman." *And you have no one else*, she wanted to tell him.

His eyebrows jerked upwards in response. "That's not—I am not questioning your abilities, my lady." His short laugh held no amusement. "I cannot afford to, after all. I have no alternative to offer."

Ruth met his honesty with her own. "You need to know I can make no promises. My teacher used to tell me that we do not heal this or any other illness. We keep the body alive until God decides whether or not to allow it to heal itself. I will do my best to bring your niece through, my lord."

Lord Ashbury bowed. "Thank you. Let me know what I can do. You sent for me; I assume there is something I can do for you?"

"I need help, Lord Ashbury. For at least the next three weeks—longer if we have more cases—the patients will require constant attendance. I cannot stay awake for three weeks."

"Of course not. Can your companion not help? Lady Zyba? Or has she not had the disease."

"Zyba has been variolated, as have I. However, someone I trust must chaperone and keep watch on the girls in quarantine. Zyba knows the signs to look for. So does Jeyhun, and he will watch the guard. The guard should not be at risk, nor should they bring the illness to your people. We separated when Anne first showed symptoms. However, to be certain, I have told him to keep apart from your staff in the stables."

"Then I shall ask Minnich. One of the maids—"

The man was attempting to be helpful. Ruth rephrased what she had been going to say, which was something to the effect: *Lord Ashbury, you seem to live in near isolation, with a handful of servants and those well past retiring age. None of them are fit to help.*

"If you have a maid who is not elderly, and who has had smallpox, I would appreciate her help. Two would be better, so they can get plenty of rest and still do some small part of their regular work. I understand you are quite short-staffed, my lord."

Lord Ashbury bit his upper lip. "I shall talk to Minnich. Otherwise, perhaps I can find a tenant's daughter, or someone from the village. What do you mean by 'variolated'? Is that some Eastern treatment?"

"It is a method of inducing a less severe form of the disease so that the patient easily recovers and is safe from infection in future epidemics." She still had the small white scar from the cut the ṭabība, the female physician, had made on her upper arm. Her brother Drew had yelled at the pain, and Rosemary, her little sister, when it came to her turn, had wept, but Ruth and Zyba had competed to show no reaction.

"Here in England," she continued, "variolation has been largely replaced by inoculation with cowpox. Have you not heard of the work of Dr Edward Jeffries? Vaccination, as he calls it?"

The earl shook his head. "I have not. Can you do it? Can you variolate my household? Or vaccinate them? Anyone who has not already had smallpox, that is."

"I cannot leave my patients, but I can do it when they are well, or can instruct you in the technique. You will need to find a case of cowpox or minor smallpox to provide the matter for the inoculation. What we have here is major smallpox. It is too dangerous to use."

"I will ask. Thank you, Lady Ruth. Though I must say you are a very odd duke's daughter."

"He is a very odd duke," Ruth said, wryly. The youngest son of the former Duke of Winshire, her father had spent most of his adult life in the Central Asian mountains of Kopet Dag, north of Iran. There, he'd married, founded a kingdom, and raised a family with the daughter of a minor Persian potentate.

He'd returned to England when his last surviving brother died without an heir, but his years away fitted him poorly for the pompous bigotry of London Society. As a duke, though, he was above such matters, and his wealth and power meant his protection extended far enough over his children that the *ton* concealed their slights and sneers behind a distant and stiff courtesy.

Indeed, Ruth's errands in the Midlands were as much an escape from Society as a favour to her brother's new wife, who was in the early stages of pregnancy and found travel difficult.

Lord Ashbury had been pleasant and even friendly. In her experience, such behaviour from an earl was unlikely. It stood to reason he had no idea of Ruth's history or that of her family.

Behind her, Jeffries called, "My lady!" The words devolved into another bout of coughing.

"Coming, Jeffries. Thank you for your help, Lord Ashbury."

The earl bowed as she turned away. "Thank you, Lady Ruth."

Jeffries needed help with the chamber pot, and then Ruth sponged her down again. The maid's temperature was lower this evening, but it could shoot up again at any time.

She left the candles and the oil lamp burning. She'd have no sleep again tonight, nor—probably—until her patients recovered. Or died. Somehow, she had to stay awake until Ashbury found her assistance. If he could. Otherwise, she would need to get Anne and

Genevieve through the crisis and then do the same for Jeffries. After that, if no one else fell ill—after that, she could sleep.

The earl's face kept intruding in her mind. He was in pain, but was it of the mind or the body? She sensed a deep sadness in him. What caused it? The death of his wife? The two girls, Genevieve and Mirabelle, had let slip that they'd not been home since Genevieve's father and Mirabelle's mother had died, three years ago. Had the earl been sunk in grief all that time? She thought of his odd hesitation when he spoke of the girls, and wondered.

3

———

Val stood by the window, looking out over his neglected courtyard rather than the other occupants of the study. Their news came as no surprise, but he questioned it, anyway. "Nobody at all? Not even in the village? Even for the money I offered?"

Minnich had been the envoy to the village. "I'm sorry, my lord. Sally Perkins would come for the day, though I'm not sure that Lady Ruth would have her. She's dirty and lazy both. Even she won't stay here the night. I told them all they were beyond silly. As if any ghosts would be here, and not in the…" She trailed off, but Val could fill in the last word.

She missed the point, or was too polite to make it. The villagers did not fear his wife's ghost, presumably isolated in the tower where she had died. They feared him; the mad earl, whom none of them knew except by reputation.

"Barrow?" Surely the tenant farmers were more sensible? They —the menfolk, at least—had worked alongside him these past three years. Many of them remembered him from a shared boyhood. But Barrow was shaking his head. "I'm sorry, my lord. It's the smallpox, and the foreign warriors, and all the rest of it. They're skittish, my lord, and nothing I could say…"

"Crick?" The butler had been tasked with asking the other servants to seek help from their families.

"Nothing, my lord. But Mrs Minnich and I have a plan."

Val turned and raised his eyebrows in question.

They had it all worked out. The three maids who had already had the smallpox would do several hours a day each, spelling one another and the duke's daughter. The footmen, who had the least work of anyone in the house, would share the maids' usual tasks between them. Maids and footmen had agreed, and it remained only for Lord Ashbury to present the lady with the plan.

When he took himself to the family wing, though, Lady Zyba refused him entrance.

"My lady says she cannot be interrupted. If you have nurses to support her, send them to me now, please. Another of the girls has a fever, and the princess is worried about Miss Bush's rash. It is flat rather than raised, which is a bad sign, apparently."

Val told her about the maids, and was leaving to send them in to Lady Ruth when he had a sudden thought. "The new patient—is it Mirabelle?" He wondered at his own relief when Lady Zyba shook her head. As he went away on his errand, he explored the emotion. He cared more than he had thought.

Ruth sat for a moment in the comfortable chair that someone had wrestled to the door of the room, and that two of the maids had helped to move before the hearth. She was less tired now that the maids shared the daylight hours between them, disturbing her rest only when faced with a problem they couldn't handle.

Ruth kept the night watch. The elderly maids needed to retreat to another room to sleep at night to be useful during the day. Besides, crisis time in a number of illnesses often came between two in the morning and dawn. Anne might face that crisis on this watch.

The girl's chest rustled. She crackled when she took a breath and wheezed when she expelled one. Pneumonia, for sure. A week from the appearance of her rash, she was fading fast, and nothing Ruth did halted the decline.

At the moment, though, all was quiet, or as quiet as it ever got. Jeffries and Genevieve slept restlessly, their fevers down for the moment, the itch of their sores subdued by lotions. The new patient —Zyba now had only Lady Mirabelle and one other in her care— was still in the early stages, her sleep racked with coughs.

Zyba had reported a few minutes ago. The two girls still in the nursery were well, though bored. The earl had tried again to recruit help, and been unsuccessful. He had offered himself and Zyba had turned him away. "I thought of putting him in my place and coming to help you, Ruth. If Mirabelle was the only one still in quarantine without the illness, it might have been acceptable. She is his daughter, after all. Though to hear her tell it, they have never met."

Ruth raised her eyebrows. The child was eight, and had lived in this house until three years ago. Still, it wasn't her mystery to solve. "I can manage," Ruth assured her friend. Zyba shook her head, but went off to bed, and Ruth made her rounds, sat to rest for a while, then checked each patient again, propping one up a bit higher on pillows to ease the cough, dribbling water into the mouth of another, listening to Anne's laboured breathing and being grateful that it continued.

Ruth repeated the cycle again and again: a few moments of rest, half an hour of nursing. She roused from a doze in the small dark hours after midnight, though she hadn't known her eyes had closed until a sound startled her awake. Something out of place alerted the sentinel in her brain developed when she and Zyba had been in the guard squads assigned by her father to escort caravans through bandit country in the mountains and deserts of her homeland. Simpler days, those, with her enemies hidden behind rocks rather than smiles and lies.

There it was again. A metallic scrape. Silently, she uncurled from her chair, reaching through the slit in her skirt for the dagger in the sheath strapped to her thigh. Against the grey of the night, a blacker shape climbed onto the window sill, pausing there to whisper. "Lady Ruth?"

Assassins do not usually announce themselves. She could probably acquit the intruder of malicious intent, which meant he was more in danger from the illness than she and her charges were from him.

"Go away," she told him. "This room is in quarantine. We have four cases of smallpox."

The man moved, coming fully into the room so she could see hints of detail in the far reaches of the candlelight. He was tall, with broad shoulders. A determined chin caught the light as he pulled something from his pocket and sat on a chair by the window. The light also glinted off a head of close-cut fair hair. Lord Ashbury.

"I am aware. Four patients, one of them my responsibility. One exhausted doctor. You need help." As he spoke, he lifted one bare foot after the other, rolling a stocking on each and then tucking the long elegant foot into a soft indoor shoe taken from his pocket. He was deft with his single hand.

"I don't need more patients," Ruth objected, less forcefully than she might if he had not moved closer so that the light touched half of his face, making the rest seem darker by contrast. Dark eyes glinted in the shadows cast by firmly arched brows. His gaze was intent on hers.

"I have had the smallpox, my lady, and I am not leaving, so you might as well make use of me. I'm no doctor, but I can follow instructions. You need sleep if you're to avoid illness yourself."

Her tired brain caught up with the comment about his responsibility. "You cannot think to nurse the girls."

"What prevents me?" Ashbury demanded. "My amputation? I have one more hand than you can muster on your own. Their modesty? You and the maids can manage their bathing and other personal matters. I can free you up to look after them in that way by lifting and carrying for you. My dignity? I work my own fields, my lady. I am not too exalted to fetch and carry for the woman who intends to save my niece's life."

Ruth turned, then, and looked straight at him, and he moved so the lamp shone directly on his face. "You are not qualified," she told him.

Ashbury shrugged. "True. I daresay half the world is better qualified than I. But I have done some battlefield nursing and I am here."

"You cannot stay. I am an unmarried woman. You are a man." A ridiculous statement. Here, isolated from the foolish scandal-loving world of the *ton*, who was to know? Besides, she would never put something as ephemeral as 'reputation' ahead of the needs of her patients.

He took another meaning from her objection, spreading his remaining hand to show it empty, and saying gravely, "I will do you no harm. I give you my word."

Of course, he wouldn't. Even if he were so inclined, he would not get close enough to try. Something of her thought must have shown in her face, because one corner of his mouth kicked up.

"I suppose you are a warrior after the fashion of that fierce maiden you have guarding the quarantine. You are three-times safe then, my lady, with my honour backed by your prowess and reinforced by the knowledge that any missteps on my part will anger your champions."

Ruth told herself her spurt of irritation was prompted by Lord Ashbury's amusement, not by the unexpected melting at her core when his desert anchorite's face softened with that flash of humour. "I was more concerned about the impact on our lives if it is known we've been effectively unchaperoned for perhaps several weeks."

He raised his brows at that and the amusement disappeared. "My servants are discreet and yours would die for you. Besides, you have your maid with you at all times, do you not? And I have my…" he hesitated over a word. "My charges," he finished.

His niece and his daughter, Ruth thought, wondering what story explained his reluctance to say the words. No matter. He was determined. He was also right; she needed someone else to share the nursing, and now she had a volunteer. Her attraction to him was undoubtedly amplified by her tiredness. Lust. A natural physical reaction, though not one she had much experience with. She would ignore it, and it would go away.

At the realisation she could finally hand her watch over to someone else, her exhaustion crashed in on her, and it was all she could do to draw herself together and say, "Come. I will show you what you need to do, and explain what to watch for."

Val moved from bed to bed, providing dribbles of water, checking temperatures, replacing or removing covers. Lady Ruth would show him the rest in daylight, she had said before retreating to a mattress in the corner and falling immediately into a deep sleep.

Lady Zyba, when she turned down his latest offer of aid, had told him that her lady was on the point of exhaustion even with the help of the maids. "They mean well, but they wake her every few breaths to check that they are doing what is needed," she had said.

She had intended, presumably, to motivate his search for a younger and more confident nurse, but Val had overturned every stone, and had even ridden into the village for the first time since he was carried into the manor three years ago, out of his mind from fever and pain. His own plea to the villagers fell on deaf ears. They wouldn't come, so it was down to him.

Genevieve had the look of his brother. Perhaps as well, under the circumstance, but it was a wrench, nonetheless. *It is not her fault,* he reminded himself, as his patrol took him to the bed where she moaned in her sleep and shifted uncomfortably under the sheet that covered her.

Every now and again, he included Lady Ruth's corner in his rounds, not touching her or even coming within reach, but simply reassuring himself that—still as she was—she was breathing.

Each time, he cursed his stupid fate. Three years in which desire had disappeared as if it had never been, and it had to raise its head now, when the object was an unmarried lady of noble birth, a guest in his home, and the main hope of the two girls who were his responsibility, as well as other people.

Fortunately, the poor light had prevented her from seeing his physical reaction, or she might have thrown him out despite all the good reasons to accept his help.

Who would have thought a woman doctor would be so lovely? Perhaps the lamp and candlelight flattered her, and the morning would show her imperfections. Oval face, large eyes framed by lush dark lashes, ivory skin with a hint of warmth in the perfectly bowed lips, the mass of dark hair confined in a plait that flicked across her buttocks as she walked across the room to the screen behind which she washed before she retreated to her mattress.

The flowing morning dress she wore should have concealed her form, but instead outlined it as she walked. He'd swear on a stack of Bibles that she'd forgone a corset, which was sensible in the circumstances, but put extra pressure on Val to remember that he was a gentleman.

Lady Ruth slept for an hour, woke to check on her patients—or their new attendant—then dropped back to sleep. It must have been close to five in the morning, the sky beginning to lighten in the east, when the knock came. Val was at the window, taking a moment in his rounds from bed to bed. Though he turned straight away, the lady was before him, rolling from her pallet in a single fluid movement that continued into a quick stride across the room.

Lady Zyba was at the door, looking nearly as tired as Val felt. In her arms, she held a blanket-wrapped child. "You will need another bed, princess." Her eyes widened as she caught sight of Val. "I regret to inform you, Lord Ashbury, that your daughter has the fever."

Ruth and Lord Ashbury settled Mirabelle on Ruth's mattress for what remained of the night, and Ruth checked her symptoms. *It might be no more than an ague from being out in the rain a week ago.* Ruth didn't believe it. She agreed with Zyba that it was probably the first stage of the smallpox.

She commissioned the earl to sit with the child while she prepared willow bark tea for the fever, with honey in it to soothe the sore throat. "Talk to her, my lord. She needs the reassurance of someone familiar."

His face went bland; a mask to hide thoughts behind. He opened his mouth, then thought again and shut it. Finally, he nodded and lowered himself to sit beside Mirabelle, taking her hand as if he feared to have it break or explode in his face.

As Ruth moved the kettle closer to the fire, and measured the willow bark extract and the honey into a cup, she listened to his low voice.

"Here we are, Mirabelle. Mirrie. That is what you prefer, is it not?

Your cous– your cousin calls you 'Mirrie'? So Minnich tells me. I am your f–father. Ashbury. Which must seem strange to you. Or does it? You have written faithfully every month, telling me your news, so I suppose you are used to me having your unc– your uncle's title by now."

Mirabelle murmured something, a husky whisper that ended in a cough. "Best not to talk," Ashbury suggested. "You write very good letters, Mirrie. Much better than mine. I can never think of anything that might interest you. Minnich does better, I'm sure."

Another murmur—a single word.

"Pictures? You like my drawings? Just silly things, really. Do you share them with Genny?"

Mirabelle shifted, stretching her neck in an attempt to see past her father, who said, "Are you looking for Genny? She is here, in the second bed from the door." He swayed so Mirabelle could look past him. "She is sleeping, and we don't want to wake her, do we? So, we shall be as quiet as we can. When it is day, perhaps Lady Ruth will let them put your beds close enough for you to see one another. You are the best of friends, are you not?"

The boiling water now in the cup, Ruth waited for the tea to steep. By chance, the room was silent, all the restless coughing stilled for a moment, when Mirrie replied to Ashbury's question with a single murmured word, "Sisters." The earl dropped the child's hand as if it burned, and flinched away.

He shut his eyes as he swallowed, his shoulders moving with the effort, then he retrieved the hand and forced a smile for the little girl. "You and she must not be afraid. Lady Ruth is a real doctor, did you know that? And you have other nurses, too. Do you remember Tiller? Preston? Carter? They are all here, and you will see them in the daytime. I will be here too, for the maids are old, and Lady Ruth has much to do and needs someone strong to lift things for her."

He continued talking, asking Mirabelle if she remembered such and such a person or animal or place, and the child stopped her restless tossing to listen to his words, nodding from time to time, her eyes intent on the man's face.

When the drink was ready, and Ruth came to take his place, Mirabelle clung to his hand, and he bent to soothe her. "Let Lady

Ruth give you the drink she made for you, Mirrie. It will take a little while to work, but it will help you feel a little better. I will just go and check on Genny and the other patients."

"Come back?" the child begged.

Ashbury gently pulled his hand from her grasp. "Yes, I will come back."

He was as good as his promise, and sat with Mirabelle until she fell asleep again. Ruth went on with her own work wearing a soft smile, touched despite herself by his earnest efforts, the vulnerability he tried to hide.

By now, daylight was more of a fact than a promise, though it would be some time before the three elderly maids presented themselves to take their instructions for the day, and longer still until the sickroom was served with breakfast.

"If you can spare me, my lady, I shall go and set up a room I can sleep in," Ashbury said.

Strangely lighter of heart, Ruth curtseyed and held out her hand. "Lord Ashbury. I am pleased to have you to help me."

His grin warmed his face, and he bent over the hand to mime a kiss, properly above the surface but so close she felt the whisper of his breath. "The pleasure is mine, Lady Ruth." Another lightning grin. "I had better see to a place to sleep."

Lady Genevieve groaned, and Ruth turned back to her duties.

Ruth was busy in the sickroom, her brief sleep during the early hours of the morning enough to put off asking for a mattress to replace that now occupied by the earl's daughter. When Lord Ashbury carried a light bedframe into the sickroom, she commented on that lack. "I will make arrangements," he assured her. He helped lift the child, mattress and all, onto the bedframe he'd placed near his niece's bed, then gave each child a smile and a pat on the hand before leaving.

She had no idea what else the man was up to until Zyba came to the door, her eyes dancing.

"Before you have your sleep, my lady, Lord Ashbury has something to show you."

Ruth looked around the room. All seemed in order. The patients had been washed, and their sheets changed. The three who were more or less conscious had been given a nourishing beef tea for breakfast. The two maids on duty were dispensing a soothing unction made to Ruth's recipe. "Go along, my lady," one of them said. "We can manage here."

Zyba retreated to the door of the quarantine room, waving her hand to point further down the hall. "Two doors down. I approve of your earl, Ruth."

She shook her head when Ruth raised her eyebrows in question. Presumably, the answer was two doors down.

It was a bedchamber, sparsely furnished with the bare essentials —a made-up bed, a washstand with jug and washbowl, a wardrobe, Ruth's trunk under the window. It was sparkling clean. Lord Ashbury was leaning against one wall and he straightened when Ruth entered the room.

"For me?" Which was a silly thing to say because the intent was clear, as was the kindness behind it.

Ashbury shrugged. "You cannot sleep properly in the sickroom, and this should be close enough that you can be fetched if you are needed."

From the hallway, Zyba made her opinion known. "This is a good idea. In the sickroom, you wake whenever your patients do, and even if you are asleep, the maids wake you with questions you have already answered. If you are not right there, they can ask one another, and only check if they cannot agree an answer."

Ashbury nodded. "We all depend upon you, Lady Ruth. What will become of the patients if you fall sick?"

Ruth found it easier to accept this practical reason rather than unmerited kindness, though she didn't agree that she was essential. She should suppress any false hopes. "There is little any healer can do for smallpox. We treat the symptoms and wait while the patient fights the disease."

Ashbury waved his open hand to indicate the room. "In that case, you can have no reason not to take advantage of this room.

Wash, my lady, and sleep. I will be just along the hall, and when you wake, we can decide how to divide up the duties."

Val was nearly ready to put himself to bed. He'd been awake all night, and had worked all morning cleaning a chamber for the lady doctor and one for himself. He decided to make one last check on the sickroom, to ensure that the maids knew to go to Lady Zyba with questions and concerns, and let Lady Ruth sleep.

He entered the room as quietly as he could. The sickest of the schoolgirls was coughing bitterly as a maid tried to encourage her to drink something for her throat. The adult patient was sleeping. The two girls Val was responsible for had reached an arm across the gap between their beds, their hands held in the middle. They lay, each on the edge of their own bed, facing one another, talking in scattered words with long pauses between.

"I met Father." That was Mirabelle. She had her mother's build: small-boned and slender, but the blonde hair could have come from either side.

"Nice?" Genevieve was also fair-haired, but with the heavier build of the Ashbury line. Val took after his mother's side—rangy thoroughbreds all.

Mirabelle moved her head in a shallow nod. "Kind. Looks a tiny bit like Uncle. But not angry. Kind, Genny." Val and his brother shared colouring, but little else.

"Did you ask?" Genny lifted her head so she could look at Mirrie with both eyes.

Mirrie shook her head. "Not yet."

Genny roused enough to insist, "He can't send us away again while we're sick."

"Kind," Mirrie insisted.

"You think he will let us stay home?"

Mirrie nodded. "Kind," she repeated.

Val concealed his wince. He had no right to the sweet innocent's good opinion. He'd done his best to ignore the pair of them, even resented Mirrie's monthly letters because he was honour-bound to think about her long enough to write a cursory reply. Now he was faced with the reality of them, he wondered how he could have forgotten that they, too, had been betrayed and bereaved.

He backed to the door again, and called, "Greetings, ladies. I am on my way to bed, and thought I would come to wish you a day of healing." The words took him across the floor to the bedsides of the two girls. He smiled at Genevieve. "I know who you are. You are Genny, my brother's little girl."

"Lord Ashbury," the child answered, hope and hesitation mingling in her eyes.

"Uncle Val," Val suggested. No doubt purists would have a fit to hear a child use such casual address, but hearing their opinion of his brother—*angry? What had the old devil put them through?* —made him determined to distance himself from the name Mirrie had known the man by. What did Genny call her father? Not Papa, Val was certain.

Genny rewarded him with a smile that tore at his conscience. "Uncle Val."

"Rest, my ladies," he told the two of them, through the lump in his throat. "I need to talk to your attendants, and then I'm off to bed, for I was up all night helping Lady Ruth. I will see you this evening, and will hope to find you both much better."

4

———————

Zyba approved of Lord Ashbury's infiltration into the sickroom. "He is not like those London idiots who scorn you for your heritage while courting you for your father's favour or your wealth," she declared. "Imagine Lord Michael in a sickroom! Or Lord George!"

Ruth giggled. Both men were younger sons whose only occupations seemed to be laying wagers on ridiculous trivia, hunting out scandal, and outdoing one another in taking whatever happened to be the current fashion one step further than anyone else.

She could not imagine Lord Michael emptying bed pans, or Lord George spending an hour sponging the forehead of a servant to make her more comfortable. In the few days since Val broke into quarantine, he had proved stalwart. No task was too unpleasant, or too lowly for his consequence, and he found a hundred ingenious ways to master things that Ruth thought might have taken two hands—changing sheets, spooning soup into mouths, spreading soothing creams on arms and faces—doing whatever was required for the comfort and support of the patients.

The only disadvantage to his help was her inconvenient reaction to him, and since he indicated no awareness of her as female, apart from his ingrained courtesy to a lady, she did her best to ignore it.

They agreed to share nursing duties at night. Ashbury took over when the other attendants went to bed, and Ruth handled the hours before dawn, with an overlap in the middle.

On the third night after he joined her, Ashbury called Ruth early because of his concerns for Anne Bush, whose lungs were more congested than ever. Together, they helped hold her head over a bowl of steam until her breathing eased.

"Go back to bed," Ashbury suggested.

"No point," Ruth argued. "The crisis might come at any time. I'll stay, but I'll take a short nap in the chair while you keep watch."

Ruth soon slipped back to sleep, waking only when Anne's cough, which had been a constant presence in the room, suddenly stopped.

Val reached the bedside a step or two ahead of Ruth, but he stepped aside to let her place two fingers on the pulse point at the base of the neck.

"No!" Ruth's protest, and her desperate attempts to rouse the girl, were equally useless. Finally, Ruth had to accept the facts. Anne was dead, drowned in the fluid that filled her lungs. Ruth stood, stretching the muscles that had become cramped as she stooped over the body.

"I lost her." She never got used to that. Patients died; her teachers had told her. She was not God, to save those whose time on earth had come to an end. But each death felt like a personal failure, for all of that.

"Nobody could have done more," Ashbury insisted.

How could he know? Another doctor would have tried different things. Perhaps one of them might have worked. "If I had taken the first shift, I might have noticed something…"

Ashbury's brows furrowed. "I missed something?"

No. She was being ridiculous. "No! I didn't mean…" Ruth sighed. "I hate losing."

He shook his head, his eyes warm with understanding. "You are a warrior, my lady, but Death always wins in the end."

He had been a soldier. Of course, he was familiar with death. She pulled the sheet up to cover Anne's face. The other patients would not need to see her in the morning.

"I will move her," Ashbury offered. At her nod, he picked the child up, sheet and all, and Ruth opened the door into the hall for him. The estate carpenter had made coffins, and they were in the next room, ready for those who did not survive. Ruth hoped that no more would be needed.

"I will put the kettle on," she said. She busied herself preparing their hot drink while Ashbury took care of the body. Who would bury Anne? Ruth could leave the details to Ashbury and his servants. She smiled. She must tell her sister Rosemary, who was scathing about the men they had met since they arrived in England. Ruth knew at least one Englishman who could be trusted.

Poor little Anne. She was an orphan, from what Ruth could gather, but the Society for Female Education and Betterment would have records of any family that needed to be notified.

Ashbury returned to the sickroom before the kettle boiled. In silent agreement, they checked on the patients, Ashbury pausing for a long time between the two Monforte girls, his face sombre as he watched their restless sleep.

The kettle began to hiss steam, and Ruth used the cloth hanging ready to lift it from the trivet and pour hot water onto the lemon and honey mix in the cups.

"Your drink is ready, Ashbury," she told him. He gave each girl a caressing stroke on her hair and crossed to take the chair opposite hers at the other end of the hearth rug.

For a while, they sat in silence. A sip confirmed that the drink was sweet enough. Ruth searched for an innocuous remark; something that wasn't about Anne's death, but Ashbury spoke before she could think of anything.

"How did you come to be in charge of these girls?" he asked. "It hardly seems a role for a doctor or the daughter of a duke." Those dark eyes, unexpected in a man so fair, watched her over the rim of his cup.

Ruth stopped thinking about Ashury's eyes to consider her answer. "Happenstance. I am substituting for my brother's wife, who is finding travel difficult at the moment." Sophia's early pregnancy precluded all but the shortest of trips, as her nausea refused to confine itself to morning, but instead responded to strong odours and anything that made Sophia sway.

"She is a patroness of a charity that funds promising girls to an education they could not otherwise afford, and the latest scholar needed to be delivered to school." Ruth had volunteered as an excuse to escape the Season. *No need to share that with Ashbury.*

"I brought Molly north, but when we arrived, the school was closed up, with only a few people left to try to turn us away."

Ashbury gazed at her intently, his expression curious. "They failed? Most people would run a mile from a pest house."

Ruth grinned at that. They had not wanted to argue with an armed party headed by a duke's daughter. "Zyba and I have been variolated," she explained. "And I had a responsibility to the other two girls sponsored by the charity."

She had suggested they should split up, some of them taking Molly home under escort while she stayed at the school, but it had never occurred to her to turn away and ignore those within. Her proposal hadn't met with favour. Zyba refused to leave her, and she couldn't send a girl child away with a group of men.

She had taken every precaution to protect her own people. Ruth had been the only one to enter the school, and she had kept her distance from the rest of the party once she and her patients re-joined it.

Inside, the school had been food for her worst nightmares. "Most of the adults had fled, and the few remaining were all sick. The headmistress was one of the early deaths, and no one took charge after that. Most families had collected their children, but presumably yours was not the only letter to go astray." Only a few people remained—the sick in one wing, and those still well in another, waiting for the illness to take them or pass them over.

Ashbury shuddered. "What of medical care?"

"A doctor and a couple of women who claimed to be wise." Ruth let out a huff of exasperation. "They were bleeding the patients, parching them by depriving them of water, and covering them with blankets—to sweat out the fever, they said. I tried to explain…" She shook her head, remembering. "They would not listen; threatened me with violence if I did not leave. I did try, Ashbury."

He nodded. "I'm sure you did. You would be there still, if they had not rejected you, fighting for the lives of all of those who remained."

Perhaps. She hoped she would. She had sworn to serve those who were ill, without fear or favour. But she would have been fighting, not just the disease, but dirt and ignorance. Yes, arrogance too, with the doctor declaring her an impudent fool, to set herself against the knowledge of the wisest of men. In fairness, he was exhausted, and he must have been a good man to shut himself into that charnel house to do his best for the dying, even if his best hastened their deaths.

"Since I could do nothing, I collected the girls I was responsible for. I was coming south again, so I offered to bring your daughters and deliver them home on the way. I feared for their survival without well adults or any way to keep themselves clean and fed." Ruth shrugged. "I could not reconcile it with my conscience to abandon them."

Ashbury reached for her hand, and raised it to his lips in a salute. "I shall be forever grateful."

Ruth thought his gratitude a little premature. They did not yet know whether her intervention would save Ashbury's two girls. "Anne and the servant who begged to come with them were both sick before we reached the county border, then Genny. As you know, Mirrie and Harmony Smith, the other charity student, have succumbed since we arrived here. Molly Porter, my original charge, did not go into the school, and rode on the top of the carriage all the way. I am hopeful that the contagion hasn't reached her. We know so little, though. I may be wrong."

Ashbury twisted his mouth in a grimace. "We will hope you are right, and that it doesn't move out into the rest of the house. My people here are loyal, but they're old."

"The old seem to be less susceptible," Ruth reassured him. "Perhaps because they have already survived this long. I think… I hope we have limited the danger." She listed the precautions she had commanded.

"Only those who have had the disease have been allowed in here. Any who enter and then leave must strip and bath thoroughly, with a strong soap. Their clothes must be boiled and hung in the fresh air to dry, and the washerwoman must also strip and bathe after touching the clothes."

Ashbury smiled. "No wonder you let few people into the quarantine, and keep them here once they arrive. All that washing!"

Was he jeering at her? "I wish to keep your household safe. And my own escort, of course."

He turned serious, immediately. "I do not mock, my lady. I know a couple of battlefield surgeons who swear by cleanliness. I owe my life to one of them." He lifted his empty wrist and let it fall again. "This was not my first brush with death. Perhaps if the man who operated when my fingers were shattered had been as fastidious as the one that sewed me up after Vimiero, I would not have lost my hand."

Ruth was torn between sympathy and professional curiosity. "It turned putrid?"

Ashbury nodded. "So Crick says. I was out of my head at the time, and for some time after. I remember enough to know I owe him my life."

Ruth caught the hint of challenge in his voice. She had heard tales of the battered and sometimes manic Crick. He was an unlikely butler or valet or whatever role he held in the house. "Loyalty is commendable," she said. "So many *sederke*—officers—think they can expect it, though they never give it."

Ashbury flashed a half smile that softened his face, but said nothing.

Ruth sipped the last of her drink and stood to return to her rounds of the patients. "Go to bed, Ashbury. Morning will come soon enough."

He nodded, but he stopped just inside the door and turned back. "Lady Ruth?" His soft voice had her turning from Jeffries's side, to be once again caught in his intent gaze. "Lady Ruth, I am glad you are here. I trust you, but I don't expect miracles from you. Whatever happens, I will know you have done your best."

⋆⟨⟩⟨⟩⟩⋆

Val slept for five hours, then woke to deal with Anne's burial. Two
of the maids washed and dressed the body, then washed down the
coffin after Val had nailed it shut. The footmen carried it to a grave
one of the grooms had dug in the corner of the little graveyard
where generations of Monfortes had their final resting place.

"We'll arrange for a proper memorial service after the crisis is
over," Val assured Lady Ruth, who watched the little procession as it
passed the sickroom window. Crick, who was to read the memorial
service, led the way, followed by the two footmen carrying the small
coffin.

"I do not know if she has any family," Lady Ruth fretted. "I will
need to discover whether someone must be notified."

"Anne belongs with the Monfortes now," Val murmured, as
much to reassure himself as Lady Ruth. His heart ached for the
poor little girl, whose short life had been so filled with loss. It frightened him to think how nearly Mirrie and Genny had approached
the same condition; how much at risk they still were.

When had he begun to think of them as his own? When he had
first overheard them worrying about being sent back to the school?
When he realised how their faces lit up when he entered the room?
When he saw the genuine love between them?

Perhaps the seeds of love had been planted as far back as when
he came to know them through Mirrie's letters. Regardless, they
were his, and he wanted never to let them go again.

They were interrupted by one of the maids with a question for
Lady Ruth, and Zyba at the door to let Val know that his senior
servants were waiting for him.

Before sequestering himself in the quarantine wing, Val had
given Barrow his authority to act as land steward over the other
tenants, and put Minnich and Crick jointly in charge of the house.
Even so, most days they had matters to report and questions that
needed his decision, so he set a time each day for them to come to
the entrance of the quarantine wing, where he would be waiting.

Today, Crick read him a letter and took the dictated reply,
Barrow expected a decision on a tenant dispute, and Minnich
gained his consent to make the all-day round trip to Melton

Mowbray for some staple goods they didn't grow and couldn't easily get locally. The visitors were making a hole in the pantry supplies.

Back in the sickroom, he was met by the news that Jeffries was struggling to breath.

"I thought she was on the mend," Lady Ruth grieved, "but now she has pneumonia."

Val's eyes went immediately to his two girls, for whom he had fallen beyond all hope of recovery. They were sitting up on Genny's bed, facing one another with their hands clasped. Genny must be feeling a little better today, and Mirrie was past the first stage of the disease, with her fever and cough diminishing as the rash came out.

"What can I do for Jeffries or for you?" he asked Lady Ruth, and was delighted when she assigned him to sitting with his girls. Mirrie had clung to him from the first, way beyond what he deserved. Genny had been cautious to begin with, so he was thrilled when she saw him across her cousin's shoulder and her eyes lit up.

"Uncle Val!" she announced, alerting Mirrie, who twisted to see him.

"Papa!"

He sat down on the bed beside them, and leaned in to give each a kiss. "How are my girls this morning?"

"Anne is dead," Mirrie blurted. She was holding Genny's hand again, and the other clutched the faded rag doll that went everywhere with her. Genny had a similar one, even more dilapidated.

"I know, my love. I am so sorry. Was she a good friend of yours?"

Mirrie frowned, as if the question had nothing to do with the conversation. "Jeffries might die, too," she stated.

"Are we going to die, Uncle Val?" Genny asked.

Val gathered them both into his arms, needing the comfort of holding them. "Lady Ruth is doing everything she can," he promised.

"We are, too, Papa," Mirrie told him. "We are going to hold one another's hands so we don't scratch." It took a moment for Val to follow the logic of the conclusion. The girls had been told repeatedly not to scratch, had been smothered in unguents meant to reduce the itch. But they probably hadn't been told why.

"That's a good idea," Val agreed. "Scratching makes the scars worse. I'd not like to see a lot of smallpox scars on those pretty faces. Sweethearts, you are strong, and you have each other, and me, and Lady Ruth, and the maids. We will all fight the smallpox. And you know I was a soldier. I am very good at winning battles."

"But Anne died," Genny objected. "Lady Ruth couldn't stop her from dying."

Most of Lady Ruth's medical care was about diminishing the symptoms: willow bark and sponging for the fever, soothing lemon and honey drinks for the sore throat, unguents for the rash.

"The body must heal itself," she had told Val, more than once. "We keep it comfortable while it is deciding whether to do so."

Mirrie let go of one of Genny's hands to lay her own against Val's cheek. "Anne didn't have anyone to love her, did she, Papa? We have you, and Minnich, and each other. Love makes us strong, doesn't it, Papa?"

Val clutched the girls closer, never more conscious of how weak he was, how impotent. For a moment, he was tempted to lie: to assure the girls that they were quite safe. But he knew, none better, how uncertain life was.

"Love gives us something to live for, Mirrie. You're right. I love you and Genny, and so does Minnich. And you love each other. That will help you to fight to stay together."

If one of them died and the other lived, the survivor would be devastated. For the first time in years, he found himself praying, an inarticulate silent cry from the heart in which the only words were, *Please, God.*

Genny was still in danger, but only until the rash began to scab over, which should be soon. Mirrie's fever and other symptoms would return as the rash covered her. At least they both had the raised form of the rash. From what Lady Ruth said, the flat form was the deadliest.

Meanwhile, the wild itch was their biggest discomfort. Even now, Mirrie's free hand was hovering over her other arm, the fingers twitching with the effort of not scratching. "Keep holding each other's hands and I'll go fill up a bowl from Lady Ruth's magic jar," he told them. That was the name Mirrie had given the large crock of unguent, whose soothing properties Val had seen demonstrated over and over again in the past few days.

One of the maids scurried over and offered to spread the mixture onto the girls, but Val insisted on attending to at least what modesty allowed. It wouldn't save their lives. But it was what he could do.

5

____

Jeffries fought for two days, but on the third night, she simply stopped breathing. Ruth found this second death less devastating than the first, partly because she was better rested. Ruth had been too tired to comprehend even how exhausted she was, until Lord Ashbury came and insisted she go to her own room to sleep.

Even more important was his command that the maids talk amongst themselves about their constant questions and worries, and only seek someone else's decision if they could not agree on an action. Then, he told them, they were to ask Zyba. If she could not deal with the matter, they were to wake the earl, who would only allow Ruth to be awakened if all else failed.

The result was that Ruth slept well for several hours each day, and again, less peacefully, for several hours at night in the sickroom. More sleep helped her deal better with everything except her attraction to Ashbury, which grew by the day as she came to rely on his help and trust his competence.

"You need your sleep, too," she had objected.

Ashbury shook his head. "You are the one we depend on, my lady. For the sake of us all, let us ensure you are well rested."

After Jeffries's death, with the others not so ill, she managed even better. Soon, she was waking refreshed in the late afternoon, ready to practice some sword exercises to keep herself in trim before taking a relaxed meal with Lord Ashbury, where they'd compare notes on what they'd heard from their respective servants.

Increasingly, their tales overlapped. Lady Ruth's entourage, sequestered in the stables until fever and rash free for three weeks, were beguiling the time with stable repairs, weapons practice, and riding exercises.

"Crick tells me that your escort is garnering considerable attention," Ashbury said to her one evening. According to Zyba, they were adding ever more elaborate routines to their exercises, to entertain their growing audience.

"Is it a problem?" Ruth asked. "Should I tell them to stop?"

Ashbury shook his head. "Not at all. Should I tell my people to stay away?"

Ruth laughed. "Mine would be disappointed if you did. They delight in showing off. But your stables are behind the house and the riding paddock behind the stables. How did your people know what they were up to?"

Ashbury saluted her with his wine glass. "Barrow tells me it took just one footman. He went with a message to the stables, stopped to watch the show, and must have told every living person he met. They've passed on the news, I suppose. Barrow says all the tenants and their workers are begging to take their break for their midday meal two hours late so they can turn up at the stables during the time your guard are most likely to be displaying their skills."

Ruth put her knife and fork side by side on her plate. "My guard are used to being busy. In another week they will be out of quarantine, as long as none of them show signs of the smallpox. Perhaps Jeyhun can find them more productive work to do about your estate. It is the least we can do, after enjoying your hospitality for weeks on end."

Ashbury had finished his meal, too, emptying his plate. He stood to clear the table, as easily as if he were not an earl; as easily as if he were not waiting on a woman. The crockery and cutlery they had used went into a bucket by the door, to be later sluiced in boiling water before the bucket could leave the quarantine, and then sluiced again in the scullery before washing. "The debt is on my side. You brought me my girls."

"While putting you and your people at risk."

Ashbury gifted her with his half smile. "You managed the risk, my lady."

Ruth shifted uneasily. The faith that patients and their families had in a doctor was a factor in recovery—a tool to use like any other to win the unending battle against disease and injury. But it never failed to make Ruth feel like an imposter, for Death would inevitably win, in the end. "In another week, we'll know if I've managed it well enough. If we have no cases in the guard or the rest of the house by the Sunday after next, we have contained the contagion."

"Please, God." Ashbury made a prayer of the words, and Ruth's soul echoed them.

"Amen to that."

Ashbury returned to the table and lifted the coffee pot, pouring Ruth another cup when she nodded. For a time, they sat quietly, sipping the brew.

Ashbury broke the silence. "Once you are out of quarantine, Lady Ruth, will you be heading back to London?"

Ruth shook her head. "With Parliament closing, the family will be moving to the country, praise be. I will go home to Shropshire or to my brother's place in Oxfordshire."

Ashbury raised his eyebrows, the ghost of a twinkle in his eyes. "Praise be? You are not fond of London?"

London was crowded, noisy, and often smelly. Ruth had found little to like, but it wasn't the city itself she objected to. "I am not fond of London Society. My Aunt Grace and Sophia, my sister-in-law, insist that we show ourselves lest people make up stories about how foreign and strange we are."

Ruth would not bring disgrace on her family for the world. Even if she never married—and at twenty-four it seemed unlikely —she wouldn't want her actions to reflect on her younger cousins and her sister. "They know much more about such things than I. Aunt Grace is one of Society's grand ladies, and Sophia is goddaughter and protégée of another of them, the Duchess of Haverford. Still, it irks me to be obliged to put on a show in front of people I neither respect nor like. I beg your pardon. I daresay that was rude of me."

"On the contrary," Ashbury said. "I think you show rare good sense." A laugh danced in his eyes. "Your retainers draw unfavourable comment, then?"

"If it were just our retainers, I think they would enjoy us as a curiosity—favour us, even." Ashbury's tenants certainly behaved that way. "No, it is me and my brothers and sisters who stick in their gullet. Even after the Privileges Committee ruled, some think that my father lied, and others are just convinced that a foreign mother —or at least a non-European mother—makes one unfit to mingle with the blue-blooded. They are fools, but some of those fools are leaders of fashion and opinion."

That put Ruth in mind of Lady Ashbury, whose aristocratic nose always wrinkled with distaste when the Winshire contingent arrived at an event she graced with her presence. Was the lady a relative? She was too young to be Lord Ashbury's mother, but she might be a second wife of his father.

Ashbury was rubbing his forefinger to and fro across his mug, his eyes fixed on the drink within. "Would it be rude to ask where your mother was from?"

"You do not know?" Ruth raised both eyebrows. "I thought all of England had been entertained by the Haverford Winshire farce."

With an upturned hand and a shrug, Ashbury disclaimed all knowledge. "I have been somewhat out of touch—at war, and then convalescing from wounds, then—well," another shrug, "suffice it to say I do not pay attention to what goes on in London. I read the papers, but mainly to guide my investments. I ignore the social nonsense."

Ruth had never been called on to explain her family to anyone. Those who mattered already knew. She paused to order her thoughts, but Ashbury said nothing, just watching her with polite— no, friendly—interest.

"The short version of the story is that my mother was the daughter of a khan, a prince you might say, in Iran, which you call Persia. My English grandfather's other heirs died, and so, last year, when my grandfather was dying, Father and most of my brothers and a sister came back to England. Our retainers, as you call them, came with us. The Duke of Haverford petitioned the Houses of Parliament to declare Father's marriage invalid and his offspring illegitimate. The petition failed when my father produced the cleric who'd performed the marriage and the man's marriage register."

Silence again, while Ashbury absorbed that. His question, when it came, was not what she expected. "And your mother? Did she not come to England with you?"

Mami. The queen of their small kingdom and the heart of their family. Sometimes, Ruth could barely remember her face, and then a word or a sound or a smell would bring a memory and it was as if she had just stepped into another room.

"She died twelve years ago," she told Ashbury. After a moment, she added, "I sometimes wonder if my father might have stayed in Vadi Pari Daisa had she lived. She always insisted she would not come to England and that Father should not, either. The old duke sent for Father years ago, when his second son died and it seemed likely my remaining uncle would have only the one heir and him sickly. He wanted Father to repudiate us all and go home alone."

"Your father refused." Ashbury didn't phrase it as a question, but Ruth nodded anyway.

"After that, though, he kept telling us that we might one day have to come to England, especially Jamie, who might well inherit an English dukedom rather than Father's kaganate—kingdom, I suppose you would say."

Father and Mami had argued over Father's sense of duty, though, even as a child, she had understood that their bond was far too deep for any surface sound and fury to do more than ruffle the surface. Almost certainly, if Mami had lived, she would have come to England with Father. Ruth gave a short bark of laughter at the thought of her mother in England.

"If she had come, she would have withered the likes of Haverford with a single glance. My mother was a queen to her fingertips, a warrior of great skill, and harem-raised by my great grandmother, who was an adviser to kings. Father says that Nano was the best politician he ever met, and Mami was nearly her equal."

"She raised a strong daughter," Ashbury observed.

At his admiring tone, Ruth's eyes filled with tears. She blinked them away. "You should meet Rebecca, my older sister. She led her own guard squad by the time she was eighteen. She can outshoot and outride most men. When a rival kagan held her hostage, she escaped and kidnapped his son, and they fell in love, wed, and now command the forces of my brother, Matthew, who remained to take over Father's kingdom. Rebecca inherited a full measure of Mami's warrior talents, and Rachel, my eldest sister, the queenly ones. Her husband came to learn statecraft from my father, and took Rachel home to Georgia to rule beside him as his wife."

Four sisters, and three of them exceptional. Rosemary, the youngest of the four, was a paragon of the womanly arts. She was an exquisite dancer, her paintings and poems were beautiful, and she navigated the fickle politics of the women's side of the house with ease and tact, so that even the most difficult of females liked her. In the more mixed society of England, she applied the same skills to the gentlemen they met. In fact, even the old duke, their grandfather, made a pet of her, and he hated everyone.

And then there was Ruth. Awkward in company, impatient with polite nothings, always wearing a mask behind which she felt uncertain and out of place. Mami called her 'my little scholar', and certainly as a child she was happiest with her books, though she dutifully took the same training in warrior craft and household management skills as the other girls.

No wonder Ashbury did not return the feelings she was developing for him.

"They are still in the East, then, your older sisters?" Ashbury asked. He seemed interested, nothing of contempt or judgement in his face or tone.

"Yes. Only we two younger girls came to England with Father. Rosemary is three years my junior. She is an artist with words, paints, and dance. My second and third brother also stayed behind, but Jamie had to come, of course, and my three younger brothers chose to do so."

"Tell me about your brothers," Ashbury asked.

Lady Ruth's affection for her family shone in her descriptions of them, and in the little stories Val coaxed out of her as they sat over another cup of coffee. It was a glimpse into a foreign land, not because of her unique heritage, but because she had clearly grown up surrounded by love. She had not been left to be raised by servants. She and her brothers and sisters were not set in conflict against one another, competing for the attention and approval of a fickle mother and a critical father.

Instead, Val gained the impression of a close and affectionate family group, with parents who were closely involved even in the lives of their younger children—those most likely to be abandoned to the mercies of nursery servants.

He had seldom seen his own parents. On the rare occasions they were in residence, he might be presented for inspection on evenings they did not have another engagement, then sent back to the nursery when his excitement made him shrill or restless.

After he was six, he was trusted to behave well enough to attend church with them, sitting as still as a mouse in the pew beside the fabulously perfumed and elegant lady he had been instructed to address as Mama, spending the entire service hoping that one of her friends might pause to comment on his presence after church, because then his mother would notice him.

His father, who did not attend church, remained a virtual stranger.

The day of his eighth birthday, the news came that both parents had been killed in a carriage accident. He dutifully donned black, but his predominant emotion was excitement that the elder brother he had admired from a distance was coming home for the funeral, and to take guardianship of Val.

He forced the memories away. Things seldom turned out the way one hoped.

Later that night, when Val and Ruth stopped for a hot drink as his time on duty ended and hers began, he asked the question that had occurred during their earlier conversation. "Have you always wanted to be a doctor?"

She paused for a moment, considering. "I always wanted to make things better," she conceded. "I used to follow our healer about, the one who served the ladies on the women's side of the house. When my mother asked if I would like more training, I was glad of it."

"Are women doctors common where you came from?" Val asked, intrigued. He'd encountered one such female with the army —the daughter of a physician who had been taught her trade by her father, and had continued it after marrying an officer in the same regiment.

Lady Ruth nodded. "They are throughout those lands. It is not proper for a man to attend a woman, you see, or even to enter the women's side of the house."

Val considered that. "Is that…? Do you mean the harem?"

Lady Ruth chuckled. "We call it the *zenana*. You English would be very surprised, and I daresay disappointed, to find that it is just, as I say, the side of the house that is reserved for the women who live there. My father had a single wife, as a good Christian should, and no concubines, either. All the unmarried women of the palace lived in the *zenana* under my mother's supervision, as did any widows. My brothers, too, until they were old enough to move to the men's side."

"But to be locked up, even in a gilded cage…" Val's protest trailed off at Lady Ruth's peal of laughter.

Her eyes danced as she attempted to compose herself. "I beg your pardon, your opinion is a common one, and might well be true in some places. In *Pari Daisa*, though, my sisters and friends and I had far more freedom than your cosseted English ladies do. We could go anywhere in the valley without fear. No one would dare the wrath of my parents by offering us insult. Beyond that, we hunted the mountains, and all of us served our turn on the roads— the foundation for Pari Daisa's wealth was supplying guards for cara-vans that travelled through the mountains. We had to be disguised as youths, to be sure, but we were expected to pull our weight."

Val shook his head in bewildered admiration. "No wonder you find London confining!"

"I find London—" She caught back what she had been about to say. "I beg your pardon, Lord Ashbury. I do not mean to be rude about your capital city."

It was Val's turn to chuckle. "You'll have no argument from me, Lady Ruth. I've never had the taste for London Society myself." Serious again, he added, "Your mother would be proud, if she could see you now."

Lady Ruth flinched. "Mami was my first failure," she admitted. "An arrow wound festered. I did everything my teachers taught me, but she still died."

Val frowned as he worked it out. Hadn't she said that her mother died twelve years ago? "You must have been still a child yourself," he protested.

"Old enough to be apprenticed," Lady Ruth insisted, clasping her hands together until her knuckles were white. "Old enough to know what I should do, but I didn't know enough." The last few words were plaintive, and tears welled in her eyes. "I did everything I had been taught, but it wasn't enough."

Val took her hands in his larger one. "Did you not tell me that all a doctor can do is treat the symptoms? 'The body must heal itself,'" he quoted. "Are you a saint or a magician that you expect all to respond to your healing hands?"

She was so beautiful. What a miserable dog he was, to be thrilling to the touch of her when she was just looking for comfort. *The beautiful duke's daughter is not for the poor broken cripple.* His body didn't care.

Lady Ruth turned her hands to grip his, and smiled through her tears. "You use my words against me," she observed. "One of my teachers admonished me for my pride, thinking my skill should be enough to save everyone I treat, whether it is the will of God or no." Her voice strengthened as she spoke, and when she pulled her hands free to wipe her eyes, Val let her go, though he ached to enfold her in his arms.

"Thank you for listening, Lord Ashbury," she said. "You have been very patient with my woes."

"I have been fascinated," he replied, hoping his sincerity showed in his eyes. "Will you not call me Val, my lady? We are becoming friends, are we not? Or do I presume? It's just that every time someone addresses me as Ashbury, I look around for my father or my brother."

"English titles! My brother Jamie spent his life as Yacob son of Yacob, then, in the last year has gone from James Winderfield to Viscount Elfingham to Earl of Sutton. He swears he sometimes looks around the room to see who is going to respond when someone speaks to him. At least we did not know our cousin and uncle, who previously held those titles. Is Val your Christian name?"

"Valentine, but only my mother ever called me by the entire name. And my older brother. I fought my way to Val by the time I was five." He bowed, for all the world as if they were in formal evening wear and meeting at a ball. "Valentine Thomas Joshua Monforte, at your service, Lady Ruth Winderfield."

Ruth reached out to give his hand a small squeeze, so that his body shot to instant attention. "Friends," she repeated. "I would like that, Val. When we are private, you shall be Val and I shall be Ruth."

6

Though Genny was past the worst of the illness, with her pox spots beginning to scab over, Mirrie continued to go downhill, her temperature rising to dangerous heights and more and more pox marks appearing as she coughed and struggled to breathe.

As she neared the crisis, Val refused to go to bed, spending long hours at her bedside sponging her with cool water to bring her temperature down, smothering the rash with salve to deaden the itch. It was a long day and an even longer night. "Look after the others, Ruth," Val insisted. "I'll stay with Mirrie."

"Talk to her," Ruth advised. "Even unconscious, she will hear you and your voice may be enough to give her the will to stay in this world."

Val was on the verge of panic at the thought. "What should I talk about?" He found it hard enough to think of what might interest the girls when they were awake, though it grew easier with time.

"Anything," Ruth told him. "Recite poetry or the times tables. It is your voice that matters."

Mirrie was the sickest of the remaining patients; Harmony and Genny both had milder cases. Val held Mirrie's hand when he wasn't actively working to make her more comfortable, and followed

Ruth's instruction, talking constantly in a low voice. He described camp life to her, discussed the planting continuing outside their quarantine and the harvest to come, recited every poem and every Bible verse he could remember, told her about the ponies he thought she and Genny might want when they were well. He talked until he was hoarse and then kept on talking, and at last the tossing and moaning stopped, and the child stilled.

Val felt her head, and the sweat was gone. She seemed to be sleeping. Afraid to hope, he said, in a loud whisper, "Ruth?"

She was at his side in a moment, examining her patient and then turning to him with a beaming smile. "She is sleeping. Please God, she is past the crisis, Val." She gestured towards the window, where the first light of day was trying to penetrate the curtains. *"Sorrow endureth for the night, but joy cometh with the morning,"* she quoted, and Val let Mirrie's hand go for a moment to take Ruth's—and pull it closer so he could press a kiss to her fingers.

"Thank you," he breathed.

Ruth shook her head. "Mirrie did it herself, and you gave her the motivation. She is out of danger now, at least for the moment. Go to bed, Val."

"I will sit for a little longer, Ruth," Val insisted. "I need time." Time to accept that his daughter wasn't going to be taken from him now he had finally found her. He didn't deserve her, or Genny either. But, apparently, he was to be given another chance.

After a while, the maids arrived, and began to help the patients who were well enough with their morning ablutions. Val let go of the sleeping Mirrie's hand for long enough to greet Genny, whose first question was about her cousin.

"She is sleeping, sweetheart," Val assured her. "Her fever has dropped, and Lady Ruth says she has weathered the crisis."

Genny ate her porridge, one eye on Val and Mirrie. As she was finishing, Ruth came to wish them a good morning. "I am off to bed, Lord Ashbury, and you should be, too. You have been up for more than thirty hours, and you will be of no use to anyone if you don't get some sleep."

"I want to be here when Mirrie wakes," Val told her.

"You need your sleep," Ruth insisted. "She may sleep half the day away, and it would be a good thing if she does."

Genny pulled on Val's sleeve. "I will look after Mirrie," she told him. "She is my best friend in the world. We have always pretended we are sisters."

For the first time, Val didn't feel revulsion at the thought. "You are, my love," he assured the little girl. "In every way that counts, you are sisters." Daughters of the same mother and sisters of the heart, even if they didn't share both parents. Which might be the case and somehow no longer mattered.

Genny clung to Val's arm. "Do you love me, Uncle Val?"

He let go of Mirrie to gather Genny into his arms. "I do, my precious. I love you both."

Genny snuggled into his chest. Her voice was so soft he had to strain to hear it. "Can we—you won't send us away again, will you?"

"Never," he vowed. "This is your home, and you are my girls. I should have sent for you long ago, and I am so sorry that I didn't. We belong to each other, and I need you both, my Genny and my Mirrie."

Genny reached up and patted the side of his face. "Go to bed, Uncle Val. I will look after Mirrie, and we will both be here when you wake up. I love you, Uncle Val."

"I love you," Val repeated, choking on the words as he tried to keep from shaming tears.

But they overwhelmed him as he escaped into the hall, and, without Ruth's guiding hand, he would not have made it to his room. There with the door closed safely behind him, he gave way and sank to the floor. Somehow, his head was on Ruth's lap, and she was stroking his head as he cried.

"I don't deserve their love," he admitted. "I've let them down. They are completely innocent, the only ones. And I tried to pretend they didn't exist."

Ruth protested. "You love them. Any fool can see that."

He shook the head that was buried in her skirts even as he agreed. "I do. Oh, I do. I thought we were going to lose Mirrie last night." He looked up into her eyes, seeking reassurance. "We're through the worst of it, Ruth, are we not?"

"I think so," she assured him. "I won't be easy until the rash has all scabbed over, but I think so."

He dashed at his face with the back of his hand, smearing the tears as more continued to flow. "I can't bear that I've lost three years when I might have had them with me, if only I'd not been so selfish, so stupid. What does it matter who fathered them? I love them. And, worthless fool that I am, I'm all they've got." He swallowed a sob, trying to regain control.

"I know you love them," Ruth assured him.

Another sob shuddered through Val, and he screwed his eyes shut as he imposed control. Ruth had not yet run screaming. For some reason, he wanted her to know the worst. "You must think me mad. I will tell you the story if you wish to hear it. It is not pleasant. No. What am I thinking? I am keeping you from your sleep."

She ran her consoling hand over his hair again. "Tell me," she commanded.

Val looked up into her sincere dark eyes, but he hesitated. "I don't know when it began. Even looking back, I can't tell. I think—I'd like to think—that their mother was pure when she came to me, but what do I know?" He spoke his deepest fears aloud. He had been in love with the girl he thought his wife was. But in the past three years, he had questioned everything. "Perhaps she was my brother's lover even then. my sister-in-law said she was, and that is why my brother permitted the marriage. He wanted to keep her close and me far away." Even that conclusion he questioned. "But Elspeth is a poisonous witch, so I do not trust her word." Ruth's beautiful eyes kept him anchored in the here and now, when he wanted to run screaming from his memories.

Ruth's voice held only compassion. "You think your brother—you think Mirrie is your niece, and not your daughter."

Val winced to hear it said so baldly. But she was right to be blunt. He could feel his calm returning in response to her own lack of horror. "That is what his widow claims. Let me start again—try to be coherent. I met Isabelle when I came home to convalesce in 1804. The Whartons were a local family, but I only knew Elspeth and her brother, since Isabelle was so much younger." Wharton was about his age, and a bullying blaggard. The whole countryside had breathed a sigh of relief when he was sent away to school and didn't return. "Her mother died when she was just a baby, and Elspeth married my brother when she was still a child, so Isabelle was raised by servants until her brother had her sent to Elspeth once she was of an age to leave the schoolroom. She was only seventeen, and a delicate little thing, but so sweet."

Ruth nodded, and the hand that was stroking his hair did not pause in its ministrations.

"With siblings so much older," he continued, "we found common ground, and soon I fell in love with her. I thought she loved me, too. Ashbury and Elspeth approved the match, and we were happy, or so I thought. But within a month, I was posted overseas."

He flinched again as a dozen scenes of rancorous arguments tumbled through his memory. "I wanted her to come with me. She begged to go, too, but Ashbury and Elspeth both said that following the army was not the place for a gently born girl."

He shook his head. He had thought he was doing the best thing, but instead he condemned his wife to disgrace and a shameful death. He gave the reason he'd been using as an excuse all these years, and it felt like sand and ashes in his mouth even as he spoke. "I left her with people who I thought loved her. I didn't even know she was with child till she wrote to tell me. Mirrie is very like her."

He had been so proud, so happy.

He fumbled for his handkerchief, dried his tears. He had started, so he would complete the whole sad saga. "When I heard two years later that Elspeth had been safely delivered of a daughter, I was thrilled for them all. She had lost babies before, I knew—four, at least, in the time I lived with them as a boy, before Ashbury bought my commission. They came too early, or they were born weak and unable to breath properly."

Val took a shuddering breath. He didn't want to move out from under Ruth's gentle hand, but he needed a drink. "My brother wrote this one was healthy, and he hoped for a boy next time."

He poured a brandy and held up the decanter to offer it to

Ruth, who nodded. Pouring one for her gave him something to focus on as he continued, "I have come this far. I will tell the rest if you are not bored beyond belief. It is not a pretty story. If you would rather I kept my peace, I will. I am recovered now, and grateful to you for listening."

Ruth accepted the glass. "I shall listen some more if you wish. It might help to tell somebody, for I think you have held this story inside for too long, and I will not betray your confidence."

Val sighed. "It is not precisely a secret. The servants know most of it, I imagine. The tenants and villagers, too, no doubt. They cannot have kept it entirely a secret: my accursed brother, his wife, and his whore."

Ruth flinched at the harsh word and Val found himself retracting it. "Or, what do I know? Perhaps she had no choice. I was far away and might just as well have been lost to her. And if Elspeth and Ashbury both… Genny is an Ashbury; no one who looks at her can doubt it. And Elspeth did not birth her, I have the lady's own word for it." He held his brandy up to the light, examining the way the light splintered through the amber liquid.

Ruth put the scandal into words. "You think your wife gave birth to your brother's child."

"That is what Elspeth claimed in the letter in which she gave me all responsibility for both girls," Val admitted. "She said Mirrie was Ashbury's, too, but I don't know if that is true."

"What did your wife say?" Ruth wondered.

Val had only the vaguest of memories of the encounter, but Crick had described it to him, and so had Minnich. "To me? Nothing. She fainted when I came in the door and disturbed them at dinner, Elspeth and Isabelle, both in their blacks, and her heavy with a child I could not possibly have fathered."

He sat in the chair across from Ruth. "I hadn't written ahead, you see. Couldn't. For most of the trip back from Spain, I was half out of my head with fever from an infection in my stump, and all I could think of was to get home. They wanted to keep me in a hospital in London, but it was a sewer. Crick—he was my manservant in the army—was sure I'd die there, so he bribed our way out and spent the last of my funds on a post chaise. The postillions and Crick had to half carry me into the house."

He remembered the familiar hall, and Minnich exclaiming as she recognised him, and the light spilling from the dining room as the two ladies of the house came out to investigate the interruption.

"Your brother?" Ruth asked.

"Had died overfacing his horse in a hunt just a week before," Val explained. "I didn't know that at the time. I don't remember anything much, apart from my wife, standing in the doorway of the dining room, the light behind her showing her shape in high relief." Val had fainted, the shock of the journey exacerbated by the shock of the homecoming.

"Crick got me up to bed and he and Minnich nursed me back to sanity again." The words continued to tumble out, more than he had intended to share, even with Ruth. "I thought Isabelle's pregnancy a fever dream, but they wouldn't answer when I asked when she was coming to see me."

He took a gulp of his brandy. Might as well tell the rest. "In the end, I got myself out of bed and went looking for her. She wasn't there. She was gone. Elspeth—gone. The little girls in the nursery —gone."

Ruth moved forward; her hands stretched towards him. "Oh, Val!"

Val turned away, the tears rising again despite his best efforts to subdue them. How Ruth must despise his weakness! "They told me the truth, then. There's an old Norman tower on the edge of Ashbury land —you might have seen it when you came from the village? She used to paint there. It is where I asked her to marry me, as a matter of fact. She spent a lot of time at the tower, especially when she was upset, Minnich told me. She went early the morning after I arrived, and when she didn't come back for dinner, a groom was sent to fetch her. She had hanged herself." He slumped into a chair, careless of the breach of manners.

Ruth put her brandy to one side, and knelt beside Val, wrapping both arms around him and resting her head on his chest. With his cheek on her soft hair, he told her the rest.

"Elspeth arranged for Mirrie and Genny to go away to school, wrote me a letter disclaiming Genny and telling me that Mirrie was my niece and not my daughter, and left for London. She lives there in the Ashbury townhouse. Well, why shouldn't she? I don't want it."

His arms closed tightly around her. "There you have it. The whole mess."

Ruth leaned back in his arms so she could meet his eyes. "You know that none of it was your fault."

Val shook his head. "I'm to blame for leaving Isabelle here. I'm to blame for abandoning the girls at the school. Three years! I've lost three years of their lives, Ruth, and I may never… Genny isn't out of the woods and Mirrie might not be through the most dangerous period of the illness. I might lose them when I am only just discovering how much I love them. I could have been building memories with them instead of hiding away here." He drew her close again, and kissed the top of her hair. "Sulking, Minnich called it, and she is not wrong. I am ashamed of myself."

Ruth's arms were comforting. Oddly, so was her astringent tone. He could trust what she said, because she didn't attempt to sweeten it.

"Well, and that is no bad thing. Shame for a wrongful action can drive you to become a better person. But you cannot change the past, and if you stay sunk in your shame, you will not change the future, either." She had two handfuls of his shirt, and she gave him a little shake. "We will save the girls, Val, and you shall love them and live with them and be a father to them."

"I might be Mirrie's father," Val acknowledged. It was enough for another gentle scold.

"What?" Ruth demanded, "You think the only way to be a father is to plant the seed? You will raise them. You. And do not think I have missed all of their talk about the letters you sent them, and the pictures." She shook him again. "You might have kept your-self here while they were there, but you wrote to them, Val, which is more than Genny's so-called mother does. The poor little lamb writes to Lady Ashbury once a month, and has never had a reply. You took the trouble to send them news of the servants they cared for and drawings of the little things that happened."

That was nothing. Oddly, he had always drawn with his left

hand—though his tutors had tried to beat the habit out of him. He made the silly little sketches because it was easier than thinking of something to say. How could that possibly weigh in the balance against his refusing to bring them home?

But Ruth would not accept his denials. "No, don't shrug. Being a parent is about the little things. My own father and mother taught me that. Grand gestures and gifts are nothing without the quiet loving actions of every day. You have made a good start, Val. You are already being their father."

She was so insistent that Val started to believe her. After all, she had more experience of family than he did. "I don't deserve them," he admitted. "But, by God, I shall do my best."

Ruth patted his back. "It will be enough."

7

———

As Ruth's guard neared the end of their quarantine, even a few brave people from the village began risking the trip to watch the daily display put on by the foreigners and their steeds. Their desire to see these wonderful warriors and horses outweighed their fear of the manor and its master.

"Mayhap," Barrow told Val, "the fools shall see thee're but human and a good man, like us farmers have been saying these three years."

Val wouldn't repeat that opinion to Ruth; she knew he'd been keeping to himself for years, but not the extent to which he had hidden away from even his own villagers. He wouldn't hold his breath waiting for local approval, but he appreciated Barrow's bluntness and his loyalty. "They'll have heard I'm locked away in the sickroom," he reminded Barrow.

"They'll have heard ye're nursing the wee ladies," Barrow retorted, undeterred. "Once thee're out again, get thee to village, milord. Drink at the pub. Go to church. There's those who've spoken for thee, but most'd rather believe the poisonous lies thy sister-in-law left behind her. They'll change their tune once they meet thee."

Val returned a non-committal answer, and said his farewells. As he retreated further into the wing to see whether his meal was ready, he reflected that Barrow was right. True, Val's few trips to the village after he recovered enough to ride again had been unmitigated disasters. He'd retreated in the face of suspicion, fear and hostility. *Drink at the pub? Go to church?* Barrow's prescription might get him strung up from the nearest tree.

He'd take it, though. He'd told himself he didn't have to care about the opinions of a village fifteen minutes ride away, but if the girls were going to live here, he needed peace with his neighbours.

Perhaps he should make his first trip into the village with Ruth's guard. He could hope some of their popularity rubbed off on him. *At the very least, they'll be handy if I need to be rescued.*

Just around the bend in the hall, Ruth was opening the door to the large empty room she used for exercise. "Good day," he greeted her. If she had no qualms about appearing before him barefooted, in a tunic tied at the waist and worn over loose-fitting leggings, he would not embarrass her by behaving any differently than if she were correctly shod and in her usual practical gown and warm shawl.

"Good afternoon, Val. I'm sorry. Is it dinner time already? I am running late today."

"Not a crisis in the sickroom, I hope?"

Ruth grimaced. "Nothing major. Just a dispute between two of the maids. They were both certain they knew how much of the new cream to use on each patient, and both determined to carry my instructions out to the letter, but they disagreed on what I actually said. By the time your Genny sent them to ask me, they were so worked up they were near useless. Genny is a sensible little thing, is she not?"

"She's a treasure," Val agreed. "This isn't the way I would have chosen to meet her, but clouds and silver linings come to mind. Dinner hasn't been called yet, by the way. I am a bit early." He gestured towards the door. "Go ahead. I envy you—walking up and down these halls is no replacement for farm work or riding."

"Join me," Ruth suggested. "A little sword work will soon loosen your muscles."

Val hoped he was successful in hiding the anguish twisting his gut, but he didn't attempt to speak, just held up the arm that ended at the wrist.

"That?" Ruth waved away his maiming as if it were a trivial detail. "You can hold a sword in the other hand, can you not?"

Nettled, he followed her into the room. She had had it cleared of furniture, apart from a table against one wall. On it, a number of edged weapons lay—foils, sabres, swords both curiously curved and straight, and daggers of various lengths.

Val was torn between admiration for their quality and nausea at the thought of displaying his incompetence. "I have never fought with my left hand," he commented.

Ruth was picking weapons up and then putting them down again. "We are not going to fight." She handed him a large sword. "Here, this looks to be about your size. The weapons act as a weight to force your muscles to work harder. And, of course, the practice steps I use are useful in an actual fight, training the body to particular movements. Like the exercises that we teach our horses. They ensure the fitness of the horse and rider, but also can be used in battle."

Bemused, Val took the sabre and performed a couple of practice swipes. It felt heavy and ungainly, and he missed his former skill with a deep ache.

Zyba entered the room. Dressed like her friend, she held one of the curving swords in one hand and a long dagger in the other. A slight widening of the eyes was her only reaction to Val's presence. She inclined her head in a graceful greeting. "Princess, Lord Ashbury."

"Val is joining us today, Zyba. Val, why not stand in front of me so you can copy what I do."

Val was slow, that first day. The two women took him through a series of movements of body and sword that left his muscles trembling, and then suggested he rest. He watched, awed, as they moved into a sequence as fluid as a dance, one facing the other, on opposite sides of the room as they continued to honour the quarantine.

They started slow, but the graceful movements of feet and arms sped up gradually, until they were moving with blinding speed, each swing of a weapon enough to eviscerate anyone unfortunate enough to be in reach.

They took it in turns to call out, at frequent intervals, a single word he didn't know, but whose meaning he guessed at something like 'swap' or 'change'. "*Calys,*" the one whose turn it was would shout, tossing both sword and dagger in the air and snatching them back again, but with the opposite hands. The game seemed to be for the other dancer—for it was a dance, though without music, fluid and beautiful—to react so quickly that the two sets of weapons rose and fell in unison.

Then *Alys-Calys*, and the swords would fly across the space between them, to be caught without either missing a step.

Val could not tell whether his deepest yearning was for the skill they showed, the hand whose loss had robbed him of his own skill, or Ruth, whose movements mesmerised him. Sore though he would be once his muscles caught up with the strain he'd put them under, he would be here tomorrow, too, if they allowed him. Even if his reasons for that were as confused as his desires.

8

___

L*ondon*
Elspeth Ashbury skimmed over the letter from her devotee in Leicestershire as she sipped her morning chocolate. Several lines down, she hissed, "What?" and put her cup down to take the letter by both hands and read again, more carefully.

The writer had a neat round hand. The words were the same on the second read.

Elspeth stood in a flurry of lace to pull the bell chain, then stormed around the room from shelf to cabinet to bedside table, looking between books and in drawers. She composed her face into an amiable smile as the maid entered. "Werther. The latest letter from my sweet little Genevieve. Where is it?"

Werther curtseyed. "I'll fetch it, ma'am." She disappeared into the dressing room.

"What's happening? Is something wrong?" The sleepy voice came from the bed.

She shushed him, and gestured for him to sink down among the blankets before Werther returned, carrying a sealed rectangle of paper addressed in her daughter's hand. Appearances must be maintained, and as long as Wesley Winderfield did not leap out of her bed naked and accost the maid, Werther would pretend he was not present in Elspeth's bedroom.

"That will be all, Werther."

Curious, she crossed to the dressing room after the maid left, and examined the room with narrowed eyes. There.

"Just a minute, Windy," Elspeth told him, her eyes on a large cardboard box, lid askew, that she'd never troubled to ask about. Sure enough, it was filled almost to the top with the brat's letters. The early ones had been written for her by some adult at the school. More recently, the handwriting had changed to awkward printing— the child's own, Elspeth assumed. Elspeth had opened them for appearance sake, but didn't read them. After all, what could a child write that might be useful? She turned the latest letter over in her hands. Franked by the Earl of Ashbury. It was true, then. Ashbury had brought the children home from school.

"Elspeth? Come back to bed."

Windy was sitting up, the sheets pushed back to show his naked form. Elspeth considered the letter in her hand and the one face-down by her chocolate pot. Half an hour would not make a differ-ence to the news, and the boy was more malleable when she kept him sated.

On the whole, he was an excellent choice. He was presentable in public, biddable in private, and totally dependent on her, since he had no money, no skills beyond a certain facile charm, and an estranged family. He also had a wide circle of acquaintances and no conscience.

As Elspeth undid the ribbons of the robe that was all she wore, her mind was already considering tactics to deal any possible threat from Ashbury's alarming departure from normal. How delightful that Ashbury's companion in scandal was a daughter of the Duke of Winshire. In brewing a furore in Society over the latest develop-ments, her lover would be a willing and useful ally.

9

Once the visitors in Val's stables finished their three weeks of quarantine, two of them rode for London with messages for Lady Ruth's family, but the other three volunteered their services in the tenants' fields, enchanting tenants and villagers alike. Val, comparing notes with Ruth, was told the foreigners were finding great delight and entertainment in the differences between country life in England and in Central Asia.

"In some ways, it is very like, Jeyhun says. Our entire kingdom is not much bigger than your estate and those farms and village properties that are under your patronage. Our people, like yours, all join together for major work projects. Yes, and for festivals and other entertainments."

Val nodded. "Barrow says he's invited your men to join them on Sunday afternoon. In summer, there's a cricket match between the village of Ashhurst and Whitley Green on the other side of the river. I played a couple of times when I was home on leave, years ago." The memory made him smile. He had been welcome in the village, once upon a time. He had forgotten that. "I don't suppose you are familiar with cricket?"

Ruth's eyes sparkled with suppressed laughter. "My father is an Englishman, Val, and had a whole kingdom keen to adopt his customs. Jeyhun is an excellent bowler, your villagers will discover.”

Val liked the sound of that. “I’ll tell Barrow! Whitley Green have been winning all summer, and my people would love to take them down a peg or two. I wish we could go and watch.”

“We’ll have to have a match when we are out of quarantine,” Ruth suggested. “Me and my people against you and yours.”

The ladies played cricket too. Val should have expected that. And, if her amusement was any indication, Ruth and Zyba played cricket the way they fought. He and the locals would have their work cut out.

“Actually, Val, you could leave quarantine soon. Zyba and Molly have only a few days to go, and Genny is losing her scabs. When the last scab falls off, she is safe to move to the main part of the house, as long as she washes thoroughly and takes nothing with her that hasn’t been boiled. The worst is over, Val. Mirrie was the last to fall ill, and now that her rash is scabbing over, she is probably out of danger. With her and Harmony on the mend, I can manage for the two weeks or so it will take. We no longer need night-time nursing, and I know you must have a great deal to do.”

Val shook his head. “I don’t want to leave Mirrie.” *Or Ruth.* He wanted to stay locked up with Lady Ruth Winderfield forever. *You could marry her.* Stupid thought. A one-handed earl with night terrors, who made such a bad fist of being a husband that his first wife hanged herself? Ruth would laugh in his face if he was injudicious enough to raise the idea.

He screwed the seething thoughts down and locked them away so he could listen to what Ruth was saying. “You can visit her,” she assured him, “if you come no further than the door and wash well when you leave. And Val? Don’t forget: if you discover someone with cowpox, I can vaccinate anyone who wishes.”

He welcomed the change of subject. “Barrow has an ear out, and will let me know if he hears anything.”

He should go. If he stayed once Lady Zyba left, and word got out that they were unchaperoned, Lady Ruth’s reputation would be ruined. And possibly with good cause. That she was his guest and had saved his children should keep her safe from his advances, but his desire for her was powerful. Between his distrust of himself and the many tasks he'd neglected—not just these weeks in quarantine, but for the past three years—moving back to the other side of the house was the right thing to do. For a start, he'd make shift to conquer his own cowardice and resolve things with the village.

Val made it to the cricket match. He and Barrow rode in with Jeyhun and his men, and Val passed the tower with barely a flinch. At first, the villagers held their distance, but then one of them asked if he'd come to swing a bat for them, as he used to, and he held up his pinned sleeve with a wry quirk of the eyebrows. "I'm not as handy as I was," he quipped. "But Captain Jeyhun, here, is a good bowler."

He took a second look at the man who asked. "Is that you, Jacob Wately? You're a sight taller than you were when we stole apples together."

The man with Wately nudged him. "Broader, too," he joked.

After that, the atmosphere thawed a little, and by the end of the day, with Whitely Green soundly defeated, he found himself part of an amiable crowd at the village inn. Conversation stayed light, though a few remarks hinted that the previous earl and countess had not been much loved. Val did more listening than talking, letting the victorious cricket team, especially the three from Ruth's guard, be the focus of attention.

He found himself sharing a table with Amos Fletcher, the village innkeeper. Not by chance, he'd guess. On a busy evening like this, Fletcher would not have sat down at all, let alone by the miscreant earl, unless he had something to say.

Fletcher was silent, chewing on the stem of an unlit pipe in between sips of the excellent local ale he brewed.

Val opened the conversation. "Lady Ruth wants to offer inoculation to anyone who wishes."

"For the smallpox?" Fletcher took another sip.

Val nodded. "Barrow is looking for a case of cowpox to give her the substance for the injections."

"Ah." Fletcher chewed on his pipe again. "Barrow said ye were not much like yer brother." He fixed Val with narrowed eyes. "He were right."

What did one say to that? What did it even mean? Val lifted his eyebrows in question and Fletcher continued.

"Ye've been fair enough wi' rents, I'll give ye that. And not seducin' the village maids. We used to hide the fair uns when yer brother was home."

Val shuddered. How many women and children did the Ashburys owe succour to? "And you expected me to follow his example?"

Another contemplative chew before the innkeeper spoke again. "Mind ye. Ye never came nigh t'village, and yer folk wouldna' talk about ye, so how was we to know ye?"

By now, all those within earshot had hushed to hear the conversation, and it was to them Val made his declaration. "I am not my brother."

Fletcher nodded. "Aye. Yer brother would'a been yellin' by now. Expected folks to bow and obey, the old earl did, and your father before him. Talkin' back?" He shook his head.

It was Val's turn to take a sip while he thought about a response and decided to push back a little. "You're a brave man. I might be more like him than you know."

Fletcher shrugged. "This is a free village and I own the inn outright. We don't depend on the manor. And turns out yer not the sort to have me beaten or to burn me out because ye don't like what I say."

Nods around the room had Val narrowing his eyes. "My brother did that?"

An even larger shrug. "His bully boys. But his orders. And he were the magistrate, so what could the likes of us do, but hide our wives and daughters, and bow, and keep our mouths shut. At least we didna have to live with 'im, like yer wife and his'n. Why d'ye suppose yer maids be old uns?"

Val had never wondered, not in the three years he'd been home. Minnich was the youngest woman in the household, and she must be close to sixty. "I appreciate your candour," he managed to say.

Fletcher grimaced. "If ye mean I call a spade a spade, then…"
He shrugged.

"I thank you for it. Honest talking makes life simpler."

Fletcher nodded, a gesture that was repeated around the room. "Aye. Ye're not yer brother. Find yer cowpox and set up them injections. Me and my family will take 'em."

"Thank you," Val told him, then turned slightly to address the rest of the room. "The vaccination against smallpox will be available to anyone who hasn't already had the disease. I'll not be forcing anyone, but I'll be paying all the costs for everyone."

More nods, and one of the onlookers spoke for them all, "The lady saved the little ladies and stopped us from getting sick. We reckon she won't put us wrong."

"Will Uncle Val be here soon?" Genny asked. Genny had chosen to stay with Mirrie, and so far, Val had visited at around noon each day, and again in the evening in time to wish the girls good night.

Last night, though, he'd warned them that he was cheering for the village cricket team and would not be back until late in the afternoon. The girls missed him. Ruth missed him, though she wouldn't admit that to anyone but herself.

She spent the afternoon wondering how he was managing. From what little he'd said, and the occasional snippet of information dropped by the maids, she knew he had been avoiding the village since his return and the tragedy of his wife's death. Would the villagers give him a welcome? Shun him? At least with Jeyhun and his men at hand, he was unlikely to be offered violence.

Their evening meal had been served before he returned. In fact, she had decided he wasn't coming, and was attempting to prepare Mirrie and Genny for that fact when he appeared in the doorway.

"How are my favourite ladies in the whole world?" he asked, propping himself against the doorframe and grinning as if he had said something very witty.

Mirrie and Genny flung themselves from the table and were halfway across the room before they remembered that they must keep their distance so Val didn't risk carrying the contagion with him when he left for the other side of the house.

"You came," Mirrie said, her face all but glowing in the light of her smile.

Genny was less forgiving, "You are very late, Uncle Val."

"I beg your pardon, my dear. I stayed after the match to talk to some of the people in the village. And now I have arrived just in time to interrupt your dinner. Should I come back in half an hour?"

Two pairs of pleading eyes turned to Ruth. Make that three, because Val, too, looked as if he would be hanged or reprieved at her next word.

Ruth had no defence again their earnest gazes. "Pull your chairs nearer to the door, girls, and you may sit and eat your dinner from your lap while you talk. Harmony and I shall enjoy a civilised meal together at the table."

Val bowed, a theatrical flourish with a slight stagger at the end. The flush and the sheepish look from under his brows told the rest of the tale. Whatever talking he had done in the village had involved a few drinks! However much he had imbibed, he showed nothing of it in his speech. The only signs were that unsteadiness when he was off balance, and a boyish cheer she'd never before observed in him, and found rather endearing.

The English used alcohol, she reminded herself charitably, the way her own people used coffee, to grease the wheels of conversation. From what she overheard as she and Harmony finished their dinner, he had conversed to good purpose, for he was assuring his girls that the innkeeper, who was the village's leading citizen, was going to help him find new servants for the manor so that his loyal staff could take on lighter duties befitting their age or retire on a pension, whichever they preferred.

"We will clean your new bedrooms first, before anything else, but we will wait to redecorate until you are out of quarantine and can choose the colours and fabrics you like," he promised. "You'll have a bedroom each and a sitting room between them. The suite also has a small room for your personal maid, and Fletcher knows of someone that he promises will be perfect for the pair of you. I'm meeting her at the inn in the next day or so, and if she seems suitable, I will hire her. If Lady Ruth agrees, I shall bring her to meet you."

He met Ruth's eyes, and smiled warmly at her nod. Ruth couldn't pull her eyes away, and something shifted and heated in his.

But the children broke the moment, speculating about this paragon and asking questions, but Val had no more information. Soon he distracted them into discussing how they'd like to decorate their rooms. Mirrie was determined on pink and frills, while Genny insisted that the colour didn't matter, as long as she could have her own bookshelf and perhaps a desk where she could write and draw.

Val expansively promised anything they wished. Ruth had to suppress a smile. He might regret that when he was sober. Or perhaps not. They were good girls, painfully well-behaved, very anxious for Val's approval, and not at all ready to trust that he wouldn't disappear on them like the other adults in their lives.

She was distracted from her focus on the earl and his girls when she glimpsed the longing on the face of her other patient. Harmony, another quiet, well-behaved little girl, was watching Val like a child banned from the kitchen while others feasted on fresh baking.

"Would you like me to read you a story from the book Mirrie loaned to you?" Ruth asked, with the fleeting thought that it would suit both of them to keep busy while Lord Ashbury and the two Monforte girls planned a future that Ruth yearned to share.

10

———

Val lived for the two hours a day he spent in the doorway of the sickroom. Not that he wasn't busy the rest of the time. He had tasks to catch up on that had been left undone during the time in quarantine. Even more important, now that he'd broken the ice in the village, he wanted to keep reminding them that he was saner than they thought, and that he wasn't his brother.

He even went to church on Sunday mornings, running the gauntlet of the entire gawking congregation to take his seat at the front in the Ashbury pew, and pausing afterwards for long enough to shake the hand of, or so it seemed, every person in the village and half of the surrounding countryside. He wore his carved wooden hand to church, but he still offered his left, and it was surprising how quickly the villagers adapted.

He spent all of one afternoon at the inn, interviewing people who came to find positions at the hall. Fletcher, the innkeeper, gave him a private parlour and kept him supplied with ale, and a substantial lunch that had Val begging for the opportunity to tempt away the inn's cook. Minnich did her best, but Mrs Fletcher's bacon pie cast her best efforts into the shade. Besides, his old retainer was going to have more than enough to do as housekeeper now that the manor was going to be home to the girls, and staffed accordingly.

The innkeeper was highly amused. "I'll tell Mrs Fletcher yer offer, but I doubt she'll take ye up on it, m'lord. Eh, but come to that, her sister might be interested. She's a widow since her man died in the war, and she cooks as good as my Clara, or near as makes no difference. Used to cook for the gentry, afore she wed."

"Will you tell her of my interest, Fletcher?"

Fletcher hesitated. He took a dust cloth that was tucked into his belt and polished the table with it. Val waited. The man clearly had something more to say.

"Mind you, she has two little girls. She'll not want to leave them."

"I have two little girls, as well," Val commented, relishing the words as he said them. "Tell Mrs Fletcher's sister that we'll work something out. Perhaps they could share lessons and play with my girls?" It wasn't a conventional arrangement, but having tasted Mrs Fletcher's pie, her stew, and her haunch of beef, he was prepared to be flexible. Besides, the sister was the widow of a soldier—or a sailor, perhaps. He owed her a trial. Any widow with two small children to raise needed the kind of wages her skills deserved.

"I'll talk to her, then," Fletcher offered. "Shall I show in the next person, m'lord?" He bit his lip, as if catching back his words.

"Out with it, Fletcher," Val commanded. "You've been honest to a fault. Don't mince your words now."

Fletcher shifted from one foot to another. "It's my sister, my lord. She wants to be nursery maid to the girls as she was to Mrs Monforte. Only… Will ye be patient with her, m'lord? And hear her out?"

The woman who entered was on the far side of forty, and thin to a fault. Even so, she would have been handsome if a sullen expression had not marred her looks. Dark hair and eyes, and little else to distinguish her from a dozen others. Except that she brought into the room a strong smell of peppermint. "This is Pansy Knowles, my lord. My sister."

Val was going to staff his place with Fletcher's extended family apparently, and he didn't mind, as long as they could do the job.

Mrs Knowles took a seat, and met Fletcher's admonishing glare with a flash of resentment. Val stifled a sigh. He couldn't have such a negative person looking after the girls, much as he would like them to be cared for by someone who had known Isabelle.

He didn't speak until Fletcher left the room. "I understand you worked for Lady Ashbury when my wife was a child."

She shot him a glance from under her brows then focused back on her hands. "I worked for Miss Isabelle, my lord."

He didn't recognise her. "Have we met?"

"Not really, my lord." She made a visible effort, flattening her tone to remove the sour edge and meeting his eyes. "I married into the village, and went back to the Hall when my husband died."

"To be nursery maid to Miss Mirabelle and Miss Genevieve," Val surmised.

Mrs Knowles inclined her head. "To Miss Mirabelle, and also lady's maid to Miss Isabelle… Mrs Valentine, I should say."

Val took a deep breath and let it out slowly, forcing back the toxic mix of anger and panic. He let the silence build until he could speak calmly. "You were my wife's maid, and you think I treated her ill, so you do not like me."

His response inflamed her, and she leapt to her feet, leaning over the table to rant at him. "It wasn't right. You should not have left her with them. She thought you would save her, take her away. Instead, you made her stay."

The door to the room opened, and Fletcher put his head inside. "Is there a problem? I heard shouting." He took in his sister's stance, the tears streaming down her pale cheeks. "Pansy, ye promised!" He sighed. "Best come along with me. I'm sorry, m'lord. It takes her this way sometimes." He had a hand on Mrs Knowles's arm before Val spoke.

"Wait. Mrs Knowles has a right to her anger, Fletcher. Let her be. I think she needs to have her say, and I need to hear her. She knew my wife better than anyone."

Fletcher hesitated.

"Go on. This is between the two of us." Val waved Fletcher towards the door. "I won't hurt her, and I won't take offence. You can leave her with me."

Fletcher looked at his sister, who nodded. She had taken her seat again, and was blotting her tears with a large kerchief. He backed out of the room and closed the door behind him.

"I am sorry," Val told her. Three such inadequate words to express his oceans of regret.

Mrs Knowles's voice was calmer when she replied. "Didn't you know what he wanted of her?"

Val shook his head. It had never crossed his mind that Isabelle was in danger from her own sister's husband. "No. I didn't. He was old enough to be her father. He'd been like a father to her."

Mrs Knowles snorted. "Like some fathers, that's certain. Been interfering with her since the first time she visited when she was fourteen, and that's the truth."

His own sister-in-law? Val had heard enough in the past week to know his brother chased everything in skirts, but a gently born child, and his wife's sister? He shook his head again, though in disgust rather than negation. "Why did he encourage me to marry her if he was having an affair with her?" he asked.

"Affair?" Mrs Knowles spluttered her affront. "What affair? Do you think she wanted what he did?"

Val could scarcely speak through a throat that wanted to choke on a scream. "Then why didn't she tell me?" he begged. "Why didn't she tell her sister?"

The maid shook her head, but she must have seen his anguish, because her voice was kinder than before. "She did tell her sister. Of course, she did. Lady Ashbury told her that men were brutes. That she should be grateful she had a roof over her head. That he hadn't taken her virginity."

Val squeezed his eyes tight shut, fighting back tears. Mrs Knowles kept talking, her voice gentle but inexorable.

"Then, when you came home and began to show an interest, she persuaded Miss Isabelle to say nothing, that she was still a maiden in the sense that mattered to men, that if she kept silent about what the earl had done, if she pretended to be an innocent, you would marry her and the earl wouldn't want her anymore."

"And Ashbury encouraged me to court her, smiled benignly and gave us his blessing. Poor little lady. I wish she had told me." His thoughts turned dark and he growled, "If I'd known, I would have killed him for her."

"She was afraid you would blame her. And you made her happy. After you were married, she felt safe, she said." Mrs Knowles smiled at the memories then her brow furrowed and her glare returned. "Then your orders came, and you had to leave. She begged you to take her with you."

"I wanted to, but her sister said… She was so young, so gentle. Elspeth had all sorts of horror stories about what might happen to her." This time, he couldn't stop the tears, though he tipped his head back and blinked as hard as he could. His voice broke on a sob as he admitted, "I thought I was saving her, and instead I abandoned her to Ashbury."

"Not at first," the maid told him. "Lord and Lady Ashbury went to London for the Season, and Miss Isabelle stayed behind. She missed you, but you wrote, and when she knew she was with child, she was happy again. He left her alone when he got back—said she was to stay out of his sight till she was decent again." She stopped for a moment, gazing over his shoulder as if seeing the whole sorry tale playing out in the room behind him. Her voice far away, she commented, "He had no time for a woman rounded with a babe."

Val's babe. Mirrie was his, and his poor wife had been as true to him as she was able. The tears fell more quickly and red rage against his evil brother warred with his own guilt and grief.

Mrs Knowles gave a quick blink, a shake of the head. She came back to the present. "After Miss Mirabelle was born, he turned out the maid he was swiving and took Miss Isabelle to his bed instead."

Val took a deep breath and let it out on a sigh. "I didn't know," he repeated, a mournful lament.

Mrs Knowles turned suddenly fierce. "She had no choice. He decided, and everyone turned away and kept silent. He was the earl and the magistrate and the landlord. What could any woman do against him? Especially one who was alone in the world."

Val met her eyes. "It was my fault," he acknowledged. "I left her. So, when Genny was born, Lady Ashbury claimed her?"

Mrs Knowles nodded. "They wanted a son, but Lady Ashbury

had been pretending pregnancy, locked away in the family rooms, attended only by her sister and her sister's maid."

The maid being Mrs Knowles herself. There was not another person alive, apart from Lady Ashbury, who could have told him the truth of it. "When the babe was born, she had to continue the pretence," he acknowledged.

The maid nodded. "They tried again, for a boy. But Lord Ashbury died. Even then…"

Val nodded. He had worked out the rest of the sorry tale for himself. "Lady Ashbury would have claimed that child too, if it had been a boy. She would have remained in charge here, and Isabelle's son would have been earl in my brother's place."

"But you came home before the birth."

"I would have looked after her," Val assured the maid.

She nodded. "I believe you, my lord, now that I've met you. But Miss Isabelle didn't know that. Lady Ashbury told her that you would throw her out on her ear, or lock her up in an asylum. At the very least, you would put the baby out to die. She couldn't bear the thought. Lady Ashbury told her she was sending the girls away to school so you wouldn't hurt them. You wouldn't want either of them, she said. One of them couldn't be yours and you wouldn't believe the other one was."

Val interrupted, slashing a hand to silence her words. "They are both mine," he insisted. "Whoever fathered them, they are my girls, and I love them."

It was Mrs Knowles's turn to lose her fight with the threatening tears. They flowed down her cheeks even as she smiled. "That would please her, my lord. If she's looking down from heaven, that would make her happy. She loved her girls." She sobbed, and couldn't continue for a minute. Val took her hand and she clutched his. "When Lady Ashbury said she was sending them away to school, it broke my lady's heart. She couldn't bear it. Balance of mind disturbed, they said, and they were right."

For a long moment, maid and lord clung to one another, both weeping.

Mrs Knowles was the first to recall propriety, retrieving her hands to dab at her eyes with a handkerchief.

Val wiped his own eyes and went to the door. Sure enough, the innkeeper waited outside. "Fletcher, would you fetch a tea tray? Mrs Knowles and I could do with a cup."

"Are you… is everything all right, my lord?"

Val managed a weak smile. "Neither you nor your sister have anything to fear from me," he assured the man.

He closed the door and returned to his seat. Mrs Knowles was composed once more and he smiled at her. "Thank you for being honest with me. I am so sorry I failed your mistress. I will understand if you cannot forgive me."

Her face twisted in a rictus of grief, and she fell to her knees at his feet. "Can you forgive me, my lord? All this time, I have blamed you as much as Them, and you lying there unconscious and like to die all the time, and almost as wounded by their evil as my lady. I am so sorry I thought so poorly of you, my lord."

The meeting with Mrs Knowles had been gruelling, but also good for him. Val hated his brother more than ever, but Isabelle's story had not only torn at his heart, but had healed it. Whether the poor girl had truly loved him, only Heaven knew. But even if Val had been nothing more than a refuge, at least she had never set out to deceive him. He no longer despised himself for believing in her, for trusting her. She was the victim in all of this far more than Val, more even than his girls.

His guilt at failing to protect her was increased, but soothed by Mrs Knowles's obvious belief that he could not have known the fate to which he had condemned poor Isabelle.

"You sound cheerful tonight," Ruth commented, when he inveigled all three girls into singing rounds of a nonsense song, and then sang faster and faster until they were helpless with laughter.

He couldn't tell Ruth how much lighter his burdens were and why. Not within earshot of three pairs of curious ears. Instead, he said, "I've hired a nurse for the girls today, and two maids to serve the nursery." All mature women, married or widowed. The young maidens were not being offered to the Hall's lord. Val didn't blame the villagers for their caution, but they would learn he was to be trusted.

"Mirrie, the nursemaid is called Mrs Knowles. Do you remember her from when you were little?" The girl frowned as she thought, and then shook her head. But when Val tried again, saying, "Nanny Pansy?" her face cleared and she beamed.

"Nanny Pansy! Do you remember, Genny? She made our huggies!" She clutched the rag doll close, rubbing her face on its tangled wool hair.

Genny thought intently. "Does she smell like peppermint?" she asked. Val agreed that she did, and Genny beamed. "I missed her," she said. "Is she really coming back to look after us?"

Val smiled and nodded, and wished he could tell Ruth the whole story. He'd have to keep it to himself while the children were around, but in less than a week, the quarantine would be over, and perhaps he could persuade her to stay for a few days.

Mirrie and Genny were released from quarantine before Harmony, the last to become ill. Their move from the old family wing to their new quarters provoked an unexpected crisis, when they realised that their cloth dolls must be left behind.

Val, who had come to escort the girls, was met with two weeping miseries, who latched themselves onto his person, their lamentations made unintelligible as they spoke into his jacket in a series of hiccupping sobs.

"I can't let them take their huggies with them," Ruth explained. "They may be a source of contagion."

Mirrie managed to gather herself sufficiently to become coherent. "Lady Ruth said everything must be boiled or scoured with lye or" —a sob fractured the final word— "b–b-burned!" The word ended in a wail.

"We will try to clean them," Ruth insisted.

Val sat on the floor with his back to the doorjamb, settling one girl on each knee, safe in his arms, their heads on his shoulders. "This is a very hard thing," he acknowledged. "Do you know why our family became earls of Ashbury?" He didn't wait for an answer. "The King could not be everywhere, so he chose his best warriors and their families and gave them the care of land and the people who lived on the land. One day, I will tell you about our ancestor, who won his earldom on the battlefield, fighting alongside a great prince. He earned a beautiful house, servants to look after him, farms to make him rich. He promised to look after them. He, and his children, and his children's children. You understand me, my girls? The honour of the Monfortes requires us keep the sickness from our people."

Mirrie sighed. "I can stay in quarantine," she offered. She looked up hopefully. "Harmony is staying."

"Just for a few days," Ruth said.

Val raised his eyebrow in question, and the lady returned a neutral shrug. It would be his decision. He was tempted to postpone the pain that few days, but it would not change the outcome. So, he shook his head. "They will have to be cleaned, whether it is today or in a few days' time. Come, girls. I promise we shall do our best to clean your huggies and give them back to you." He hugged them closer and pressed a kiss to each little head. "Let me escort you to Nanny Pansy, who is waiting with your baths."

They made no further complaint, but let him lead them, two subdued little shadows, to the room where baths had been set up ready for them. It was a relief to hand them over to Nanny Pansy, who greeted them with tears and hugs, and declarations of love.

Val went to his own bath. What would happen to the two rag dolls when they were boiled? At the very least, their painted faces would run, and the hanks of wool that made up their hair would shrink and mat into felt. Still, it had to be tried.

11

———————

Ruth did not expect to see Val again that day. With the girls out of quarantine, he had no reason to visit the wing. But not long after Harmony settled to sleep, there was a tap on the sickroom door, and there he stood.

"Val! Is something wrong?"

He grinned. "Something is right. Nanny Pansy made the huggies, and she assures me they're stuffed with cotton rags, and have survived the boiling. They looked awful to me, but she tells me she can reshape them and give them new faces and new hair. She has Mirrie and Genny all excited, because I have said the girls are to have all new wardrobes, and Nanny Pansy says she will make new matching wardrobes for the dolls."

He ran out of confidence and words, and looked down at his feet. "I am sorry. I have disturbed you." He met her eyes. "I just thought you might like to know. Good night, Ruth."

Ruth put out a hand towards him. She was too far away to grasp his arm, and would not be able to, in any case, while she was still in quarantine and he was out. "Don't go. That is… If you don't have somewhere else you need to be?" *Fah!* She navigated the hostile drawing rooms of the *ton* with a chilly ease that earned her the sobriquet 'North Wind', but completely lost her composure with this man.

He turned back towards her, his eyes warming. "Nowhere I would rather be." A quick shake of the head and a short laugh, and he amended that statement. "Nowhere I would rather be tonight, though I could wish you were free of quarantine, and we could take a walk. It is a warm evening, with a bright moon. My mother's white garden has been neglected, but it is still full of blooms that gleam in the moonlight. She chose many of them for their scent. I would like to show it to you."

"I would like that. The moon is not yet full. May we hope for a fine evening one night after I leave quarantine?"

He rewarded her with a glowing smile. "Barrow says the weather will hold for at least a week." He waved a dismissive hand. "It is still attractive in the daytime, even in the rain. But a fine moonlit night— Isabelle used to say it was the most romantic place in the world."

It was the first time she had seen Val speak of his deceased wife without a shudder. But even as she had the thought, he commented, "Mrs Knowles—Nanny Pansy—was devoted to my wife, and—so I understand—something of a confidante. May I share with you what she told me?"

If it was something that gave Val ease, Ruth must be glad for him, and this wave of jealousy against a woman three years dead, and in such tragic circumstances, was quite uncalled for. And they were, for all intents and purposes, alone—in a wing that only contained the two of them, a sleeping child, and the remaining two maid-helpers, also asleep. "Of course," she replied.

She sat inside the door, and he sat outside and told his sorry tale. It seemed the former Earl of Ashbury was a rakehell care-for-naught of the most dishonourable kind. Poor Isabelle. Yet knowing the truth had clearly helped Val.

Even as she had the thought, he said, "I bleed inside to think how badly I failed that poor girl, and yet, at the same time… Is it awful of me to be glad that she would have been true if she could? Somehow, knowing she was a victim of my brother and her sister relieves my heart. I can remember her as a sweet young woman, kind and gentle."

"I understand that," Ruth said. "You can grieve her properly, now."

This time, his smile was wistful. "I have mourned long enough, I think. I can honour her best by making sure her daughters are given the love and the family she and I lacked. What you've said about your family gives me inspiration, Ruth. I'd like very much to give my girls memories like yours. Thank you for sharing them with me."

Ruth's heart turned over in her chest. How did the selfish, grasping despot who preceded him and this dear, sweet, honourable man come from the same parents? "It has been my pleasure, and I hope you will have the opportunity to meet some of them." She would have caught the words back if they had not already flown her lips. He might believe she was angling for a courtship, which she would never do, much as she might be open to one. But he was nodding.

"I would like that very much."

She talked about her family, prompted by his eager questions. When he asked the meaning of the name of her father's valley kingdom, *Vadi Pari Daisa*, she translated it for him.

"Paradise Valley, you would say. A *pari daisa* is an enclosed garden, and my parents named their kingdom for the mountains that ringed it, and also for my mother's garden, which my father gave her as a wedding gift. It is one of my favourite places in the world. In the summer, it was ablaze with colour. Even in the winter, when the snow sat deep, we would sit in the pavilion when the sun shone, warmed by braziers, enjoying the peace. My brother's wife maintains it now, and holds court where my mother used to. If I could take you anywhere in space and time, it would be to the Queen's garden, when my mother was queen."

Val had been listening with devoted attention, his eyes fixed on her lips. Or perhaps his mind was on the present rather than history, because he murmured, "Any place you are is Paradise to me." He winced and blushed. "I beg your pardon. I did not mean to say that."

"Perhaps it is time for bed," Ruth suggested, wishing she could be as brave. She hoped the warmth of her smile might hint at her wish for more such compliments. It may have helped, for Val mimed bowing over her hand in farewell, and his step as he strolled away down the hall was positively jaunty.

The freshened huggies were a great success. Mirrie and Genny were proud to display them when Val went up to the nursery to join them for nursery tea. Not that he could see much beyond their freshly painted faces and heads adorned with brand-new wool wigs, one bright yellow and one black. Each doll was wrapped firmly in flannel.

"They have to remain wrapped in blankets, Papa, until their clothes are made," Mirrie explained.

Val was concerned that the change in hair colour might distress his girls—the previous hanks of wool had been a dull brown. But Genny assured him that each girl had chosen for her own doll, and if they were happy, as he told Ruth when he visited after dinner, he was happy. "Oh, and Nanny Pansy will make one for Harmony, if she wishes. If she is not too old for it at nearly ten. Molly declares that eleven-year-olds do not need rag moppets."

"I will ask her in the morning," Ruth assured him.

Again, they talked for more than an hour, and finished on a high note, when Ruth said, "Will the weather be fine tomorrow evening, according to your local weather prophet?"

"Tomorrow evening?"

Ruth smiled, her eyes full of warmth. "I expect Harmony's last scab to be gone by morning."

It was, too. Mrs Minnich had been making plans with Zyba and Ruth. As soon as word came from the quarantine wing, she sent for reinforcements in the village, and a whole battalion of locals descended on the hall. Everyone who could be spared within a five-mile radius was ready to scrub, boil or burn everything that may have come into touch with the smallpox.

By the time they arrived, Harmony had been bathed thoroughly, moved to the same wing as the other girls, and greeted with enthusiasm. Ruth remained, directing the work inside the house, while Val took station outside to make sure that her instructions were carried out to the letter.

It took most of the day, but finally the last of the day workers took their payment and a bundle of food for their families, and set off home. Val went up to the nursery, and found Ruth and Zyba had arrived before him. He stopped in the doorway. She was dressed for dinner rather than in the practical day gowns he was used to seeing, and looked every inch the daughter of a duke.

Still, she was seated on the floor, with Mirrie and Genny one each side of her. Zyba sat facing her a few feet away, with Harmony on one side and Molly on the other. He craned to see what they were doing, unwilling to move from the doorway in case he disturbed them.

But a moment later, the tableau was broken, as Mirrie spotted him and leapt to her feet, running towards him. "Look, Papa. Lady Ruth has been teaching us to make shadows."

He caught her wildly waving hand in his, his heart thudding. "No running with scissors, child." Her face collapsed at his barked reprimand, and she wriggled, pulling away.

Genny abandoned what she had been doing to fling herself to her cousin's defence. "Let go of her. You are hurting her," the girl yelled, pulling on Mirrie's wrist and then on Val's handless arm, but Val was afraid to release Mirrie's hand, lest the sharp point of the scissor blades hurt one of his girls. He forced his voice to calm. "Don't be frightened, Mirrie, my love. Hold still. Give me the scissors." Mirrie had dissolved into terrified sobbing and didn't hear him, but Ruth reached them and took Genny into a hug, kneeling behind the girl and pulling her onto her lap.

"Your uncle is trying to help Mirrie," she murmured. "Trust your Uncle Val."

With the weight on his arm removed, Val was able to coax the scissors from Mirrie's hand, and the crisis was over. He handed the implement to Nanny Pansy, sharp points down so that she could wrap them in her palm. "Mirrie. Mirrie, it's all right. I'm sorry I shouted. I was frightened you might fall and hurt yourself on the points." By now he had enfolded her in his arms and she had softened to cling to him, sobbing on his shoulder. Not for the first time, he wondered what his girls had endured to make them so nervous.

He held out an arm for Genny, and she disentangled herself from Ruth to hug him and Mirrie. "We made shadows," she told Val. Mirrie unscrunched her other fist and burst into tears again. "I have broken my shadow!" she wailed. The paper shape in her hand was rumpled and torn.

"Then you shall make another elephant to show your father," Ruth declared, then faltered, looking at Val as she added, "if you do not object. She is usually very careful with the scissors, Lord Ashbury."

Val cupped a hand around each girl's face in turn, Mirrie first, drawing them to look at him. "Of course, you may use scissors to make shadow pictures. Mirrie, you must always put them down, as Genny did, before you hurry across the room. And if you are walking, walk carefully. I will show you how to hold them safely."

"You handled that well," Ruth said later, as he escorted her in to dinner.

"I frightened them," Val objected.

"They will remember the lesson all the better. You soothed them after."

They were dining with Zyba and Jeyhun, who—as far as Val could figure—stood more in relation to his lady as medieval knights to their sworn lord than as modern-day servants to an employer. Once they sat, the conversation became general. The messengers had returned from Ruth's family, with letters calling her home. "Winds' Gate in Shropshire first," she said, "and then perhaps Oxfordshire, with Sophia and James, or possibly Brighton, where Father has taken a house for the summer."

Val swallowed a lump. "When must you leave?"

"In a few days," Ruth said. Zyba and Jeyhun exchanged a startled glance, but made no comment. "Can you be ready by Monday?" Ruth added, raising one brow at her guard commander.

Jeyhun inclined his head. "We can be ready in the morning, princess."

"I could do with several nights of uninterrupted sleep, I have yet to carry out my promise to vaccinate your villagers, and I would like to attend church in your village." A hint of mischief twinkled in her eyes as she looked up at Val across the table from her. "Besides, you promised me a tour of your white garden."

"After dinner?" Val suggested.

And then, of course, Zyba and Jeyhun wished to know about the white garden, and expressed an interest in seeing it. Val could think of no reason to deny their request; no reason that might not get him gutted for his impure thoughts about the duke's daughter, that is. And so, after dinner, all four of them repaired to the little walled paradise that Val's mother had once loved so dearly.

Had she not been equally frustrated, Ruth might have been amused at Val's valiant attempts to hide his dissatisfaction with the additions to their company. She had planned to allow him the kiss she hoped he wished to steal.

Her spirits soared, however, when they came through the gate into the enclosed space. It was larger than she expected, larger even than her mother's garden. It was also very overgrown, so that one path could not be seen from another. And Jeyhun and Zyba had been courting in decorous fashion for some time.

She bided her time, allowing Val to conduct the tour of the main features of the garden. Despite his constant refrain of, "Of course, it used to be much more beautiful," enough remained to charm and delight. The former Lady Ashbury had selected for scent and form, as well as for plants whose blooms were open at night, and all the blooms were white, glowing luminescent in the light of the moon, as did much of the foliage.

At last Ruth suggested sitting for a while on a bench near the central fountain. As she expected, her captain and her companion quickly became restless. They had been comparing eastern gardens with the ones they had seen since their arrival in England, and Zyba was certain that a tree they had passed near the entrance to the enclosure was similar to one that bloomed in a garden they had visited in Istanbul. Jeyhun was equally sure she was mistaken.

"Why do you not go and take another look?" Ruth asked.

Jeyhun opened his mouth to argue about leaving her alone with their host, but Zyba took his arm and led him away. Val looked at Ruth with what she was certain, even in her innocence, was desire, but he stayed sitting on the rim of the fountain.

"There is plenty of room beside me," she said, her cheeks heating at her own boldness.

He leapt up and closed the space between them in two long strides, then sat just far enough away that he touched no part of her, except for the heated gaze that swept from her brow to her shoulders, bared by the fashionable gown, and lower.

She returned the gaze, tracing his face, his shoulders, his torso, with her eyes, and when he leaned towards her, she met him partway. Only their lips touched, brushing once, twice, a third time. He straightened, so that his face drew away a few inches. "Ruth?"

She answered what she hoped he was asking. "Yes." She leaned towards him again, and he shifted so that they were thigh to thigh. He slid his hands—flesh on one side and carved wood on the other—across her arms and around her back, pulling her chest to chest. This time, when their mouths connected, they clung.

She was vaguely aware of the texture of his jacket under her palms, but most of her attention was on the touch of his lips on hers, of his teeth nipping her lower lip, of his tongue surging inside her mouth when she gasped at that gentle nibble.

She turned her face to give him better access. She had always wondered whether noses interfered with kissing, but apparently her body knew how to prevent that from happening. Someone moaned, and she rather thought it was her. Without her willing it, her body moulded itself to his, but she could not get close enough. She edged up onto his thigh, and it was his turn to moan as her leg slipped down between his and pressed up against something rigid and unyielding.

"Ruth…" he said her name on a groan, then again, this time more sharply, turning his head as her mouth followed his and tried to reconnect. "Ruth. Sweetness. We have to stop."

Yes. Yes, they did. Heavens! Jeyhun and Zyba were somewhere nearby, perhaps just around the corner, and she was draped over the

Earl of Ashbury like a tavern slattern. She jerked away from him, the heat rising in her face. Whatever did he think?

"I beg your pardon," she murmured.

"I am the one that should apologise, but I find it hard to be sorry. That kiss…!" Val's voice still sounded strained, as if he were in pain. Her doctor's mind registered a point from her reading: extreme tumescence could be painful, and when she had been on his lap, she had felt his… If her face got any hotter, it would melt.

She opened her mouth to make some sort of an excuse for her behaviour, or to change the subject to something innocuous. But what came out just added to her embarrassment. "I have never been kissed before. Was it…?" She wasn't sure what she was asking. *Was it exceptional? Was it meaningful to you? Was it something we could do again?* Perhaps all of them.

Val, who had dropped his arms when she shifted away, lifted his good hand to cup her cheek and move her face so he could gaze into her eyes. "I have never had a kiss like that in my life. Ruth, you are an exceptional woman, and make me wish with all my heart I was a better man."

She leaned into his hand. "You are a good man, Valentine Monforte."

A burst of dialogue came from just beyond the hedge that shielded them. Jeyhun and Zyba were returning.

Val caressed her lips with his thumb before standing, allowing his fingers to trail over her cheek as he dropped his hand and stepped away. He was just in time. Jeyhun and Zyba rounded the turn in the path, and their stolen moment together was over.

12

———

Val had a restless night, reliving that kiss and trying not to dwell on taking it further. His conscious mind was hard enough to redirect. Asleep, his libido had free rein, and he woke more than once, sweaty and aroused, in a tangle of sheets, a naked Ruth fading from his arms as his dream dissipated.

He'd come downstairs for breakfast, to the news that Barrow had at last found a case of the cowpox for Lady Ruth's inoculations. She immediately began planning. The first step would be to examine the patient to confirm that the case was, indeed, cowpox. "People have died before now because the patient from whom the material for inoculation was collected had a mild dose of smallpox, and not cowpox at all," she explained.

Immediately after breakfast, she rode off with Barrow, escorted by Zyba and one of the guards. Val would have gone too, but he had his orders. Ruth was sending him to put out word that the vaccinations would start tomorrow.

He returned home shortly after midday, ready to report progress. "Is Lady Ruth back?" he asked Crick, as he handed the man his outwear.

"She is in the drawing room with her gentleman caller," Crick replied, his voice stiff with outrage.

Val's own hackles lifted, though he had no right to be jealous. After all, one kiss, however splendid, did not make her his. Even the idea was ridiculous. She might have submitted to a single embrace, influenced, no doubt, by their forced proximity in the past few weeks and the power of the moonlight. But surely, she could have no true interest in a crippled recluse, haunted by his failures as a husband and a father. Certainly, she could do much better.

Even so, he entered the drawing room as silently as he could, hoping to see the visitor before he was seen. The man sat side by side with Ruth on a sofa near the window, and a single glance was enough to settle Val's agitation. Everything about them disclosed their relationship—this was one of her brothers.

The hair was the same shade, and they shared eye colour and the shape of cheekbones and brows, allowing for differences between men and women. But beyond that, there was nothing of desire in their body language or the way they looked at one another. Ruth's gaze on the man was fond and familiar, but not intimate, as he said something in a low voice, his eyes dancing and half a grin curling the corner of his lips. Whatever it was, she slapped his thigh, causing him to yelp and comment, loud enough for Val to hear, "Proper English ladies do not resort to violence!"

"Rubbish, Drew, what do you know of proper English ladies?" She smiled at Val, and he approached to be introduced. "Val, come and allow me to make known to you my scapegrace brother, Lord Andrew Winderfield. We call him Drew."

The brother stood and held out a hand for Val to shake, and showed no hesitation in grasping the left hand Val extended; indeed, no reaction at all beyond a swift glance at the empty wrist on the right. He was almost as tall as Val, and casually dressed in riding clothes, still somewhat dusty from his travels. English tailoring rather than the Turkmen coats that Ruth's guard preferred, though the silk of his colourful waistcoat was an exotic weave reminiscent of an oriental carpet. Something about his eyes hinted at an origin further east than Persia. Did he and Ruth have Chinese blood?

"Lord Ashbury," he said, "I came to escort my sister home, but she tells me she has inoculations to carry out in the next two days. May I impose on your hospitality until she is ready to travel?"

"Drew!" Ruth exclaimed. "How rude!"

"Not at all." Val sent her a quick smile, and then addressed his reply to Lord Andrew. "After the service that Lady Ruth has rendered me and mine, I am pleased to give any member of her family freedom of my lands and hospitality under any roof I can call my own." Even if the presence of a brother would make it infernally difficult to steal another kiss. Not that he should. He stopped himself from casting Ruth a yearning look. The last thing he needed was to annoy any member of her family. Undoubtedly, for all his amiable smile, Lord Andrew was as formidable a warrior as his sister and her retinue.

Lord Andrew invited Val to call him Drew, and proved to be an easy guest, happy to lend a hand with preparing the vaccine, charming to the little girls when they joined the adults for afternoon tea, and entertaining over dinner, when he and Jeyhun competed to tell stories of their own apprenticeship as guards on caravans passing through the mountains at the Persian end of the Silk Roads. Just as well it was raining that night, saving Val from the sin of resenting his guest's chaperonage of Lady Ruth, since they had no opportunity to stroll again in the White Garden.

The following day, when they all trooped down to the village to carry out inoculations, Drew rode one of the three horses he'd brought with him, all prime examples of the Turkmen breed that the guard rode, brought with the family and their followers from *Vadi Pari Daisa.*

Ruth set him and a couple of the retainers to entertaining those waiting around the front of the inn, where Fletcher had given over the front parlour for Ruth to use as a clinic. Val was kept busy renewing his acquaintance with villagers he knew from his childhood and meeting new ones, but didn't miss the evidence that he was right about Drew's skill. In riding, sword play, and hand-to-hand combat, the friendly young lord easily met or bested Ruth's most skilled men.

The second site of the day was a small hamlet north of Val's estate. The local tavern had turned its customers out onto the benches that looked over the green, and Ruth set a couple of maids to scrubbing the area she'd use in the large public room where drinks were normally served.

The crowd gathering to be vaccinated was much smaller, and they were on their way in under an hour. The last stop of the day was the home of the baronet who served as the district's magistrate and Master of the local hunt.

Val had met with Sir William the day before, and was pleased to find that the older gentleman had carried out the instructions for preparing the clinic to the word. He could see through wide-open doors that the carriage barn had been cleared and cleaned, with scrubbed tables and boiling water ready to hand. Only one element was missing. Where were the patients?

Sir William stood alone in the stable yard before the barn, his normally amiable face drawn into a scowl.

"Sir William," Val greeted the man as they dismounted.

"Ashbury. I need to tell you…"

The baronet had shot one fearsome scowl at Lady Ruth and then turned his head. Val's instincts pricked, and he rushed into speech before Sir William could finish the sentence.

"Lady Ruth, Lady Zyba, may I have the honour of presenting to you the district's King's man, Sir William Harwood, who has given his full support to this effort to protect our people. Sir William, Lady Ruth is also accompanied by her brother, Lord Andrew Winderfield."

Drew put out a hand for Sir William to shake. For a moment, Val was afraid that the baronet would refuse it, and he breathed out in a sigh when Sir William returned the clasp. "Her brother, you say?" Some of the tension left him. "You have the look of one another, at that. And you are staying at Ashcroft Hall as well?"

Drew offered a shallow bow in Val's direction. "Lord Ashbury has honoured me with his hospitality, yes."

Sir William fixed his intense stare on Ruth. "Ashbury here insists you know what you are doing with this cowpox. What does a duke's daughter know about medicine?"

What was Sir William up to? Val had explained her skills and her training when he first asked the man to organise this part of the district. Ruth put a hand on Val's arm when he would have responded angrily.

"What are your concerns, Sir William?"

"You are a woman." The man gave a sharp nod, shaking off any momentary doubts. "A foreign woman, I have been told, and I can see with my own eyes, it is true." His eyes swept from her to the retainers in their exotic tunics and large sheepskin hats. "I suppose if your brother has been with you the whole time, I might discount the accusations that you and Ashbury here are lovers. Even so, I don't feel right trusting a female with the welfare of my servants and tenants, let alone one who practices who knows what foreign tricks."

Ruth spoke before either her brother or Val could respond to the nonsense. "It is apparent someone has spoken against me since Lord Ashbury was here yesterday. May I face my accuser?"

Sir William looked up at the house, and Val followed his gaze. A woman was watching them from a window on the second floor. The glass and the distance distorted her face so Val couldn't be sure, but he would lay odds that it was Lady Harwood, the baronet's wife, a contemporary and friend of Elspeth's. Was she the source of the man's reluctance?

He acted on the assumption, drawling, "I take it your wife corresponds with my sister-in-law. I suggest you warn her not to listen to or promulgate malicious gossip."

"I second that recommendation," Drew agreed. "Making enemies of the Duke of Winshire and the Earl of Ashbury seems unwise."

Sir William reddened. "Are you threatening me, young pup?"

Drew was about to say something else, but Ruth interrupted. "Gentlemen, we are wasting our time here. Sir William, I hope you and your people do not live to regret your refusal to avail yourself of Dr Jenner's protection against smallpox."

She mounted and was turning her horse as Sir William stepped forward and grabbed at the reins, spluttering, "Another threat! Do you plan to curse them? Are you a witch?"

He missed the reins as Ruth's horse danced sideways, tossing its head high, and Drew and Val crowded in on the idiot, one from each side. Val hadn't seen Drew draw a dagger, but it was pressed to

Sir William's throat, and all the colour had drained from the man's face.

"You fool," Val hissed. "Lady Ruth makes no threats. She offered to protect you and your people from smallpox, and you have rejected that offer. When the disease recurs in this district and my people are safe, remember that you had a choice. Let him go, Lord Andrew. He's not a danger to your sister. We're leaving."

Drew removed the knife, just a little, but Sir William was an even bigger fool than Val realised. Even with the threat still present, he snarled at Drew. "I'll have you arrested, drawing a knife on the King's man. I'll have you locked up and throw away the key."

Val didn't expect Drew's shout of laughter. "By all means try. I will explain to the Prince Regent when I next see him that the magistrate of this county attacked my sister. His Highness has a great respect for Lady Ruth since she gave him advice on management of his gout."

The sound of voices attracted their attention to the house. Double doors had been opened into the garden, and Lady Harwood was just outside, haranguing a crowd of figures still on the other side of the doorstep. From what Val could see, they comprised half a dozen footmen armed with brooms and kitchen knives, none of whom seemed keen to attempt a rescue of their master.

"Come," Ruth called, from the corner of the stable yard that gave access to the driveway. Most of the party had followed her; only Val and Drew remained. Val mounted his horse, and after a moment's hesitation, Drew whistled a signal to his, and leapt over its haunches and into its saddle as it stepped after its brethren.

He turned back then, lifting a brow. His usual amiability dropped away to leave the warrior's face, stark with menace as he addressed Sir William, "Do not attempt to follow us, keep away from my sister, and control your wife."

13

The vaccinations the next day were scheduled in the great room of the rectory after church. Val went to the service with his girls and the Winderfield party, and was pleased with the welcome they got in the churchyard after the service. The Harwoods did not attend.

The vaccinations went without a hitch, and on the following day the Winderfield contingent left. The four girls were in tears at the parting. Mirrie and Genny had tried to convince Val that two extra girls would be no trouble for him, and couldn't possibly comprehend why he balked at bringing another two innocents, and these no relation, into his scandal-tarnished life.

Harmony and Molly were heading for a new school, and were nervous about the change, though Ruth assured them that Lady Sutton planned to keep them together, and that Ruth would keep in touch and visit when she could.

Since Drew arrived, Val had not had a private moment with Ruth. He seized a moment to draw her to one side when his girls suddenly thought of one more item for their friends' comfort, and obtained permission to race upstairs to the nursery to retrieve a travelling games-set to help while away the journey.

Val kept his voice low, though Drew, Zyba, and Jeyhun were exchanging banter as they waited, and not paying attention to Val's conversation with Ruth.

"Thank you for my girls."

Ruth shook her head. "I had little to do with it, Val."

Val caught up her hands, unable to resist this last chance to touch her. "I don't believe that. You say your job is just to treat the symptoms while they heal themselves. Well." He kissed one hand, and then the other. "You have treated their symptoms. You haven't starved them or bled them. And they live. Thank you."

Ruth blushed; whether at his kisses or his words, he didn't know. "I didn't save Jeffries or Anne."

"Three from five live," Val pointed out. "I've seen smallpox go through a village and kill nine out of every ten. You'll let me be grateful, Ruth. Grateful, too, that you imposed a strict quarantine, so it hasn't spread beyond those who brought it with them. And that you've saved those who might have caught the disease in the future."

Ruth still wouldn't accept how wonderful she was. "It was the least I could do, Val. I brought the smallpox here. And we have been lucky. Only one of them had one of the more dangerous forms of the disease, praise God."

The girls came clattering back down the stairs, and Drew called out, "Ruth, time for us to go."

It was over, then. She had come into Val's life and changed everything. If only he were a different man, a whole one not mired in a disastrous family history. An earl might aspire to a duke's daughter, if he were worthy. He had seen a glimpse of a blissful future, but only through the bars of the cage that kept him from ever enjoying it.

As he watched the carriage and riders disappearing down the drive, and comforted his weeping girls, he swallowed a lump in his own throat, and blinked hard.

"Lady Ruth promised to write," he reminded Genny and Mirrie. And Val would have to take what comfort he could from the letters she sent to his girls.

"Shall we see if Cook has cake and milk?" He escorted the girls to the kitchen to make the enquiry. As they sat with large slices of chocolate cake, giggling at the milk moustaches they'd each managed to fit themselves with, Val had to smile, too.

It hurt to say goodbye to the only friend he'd had since he left the army, but—on the other hand—he was no longer alone. Even in his grief, his girls brought him moments of joy. *Ruth has left me better off than I was before she came.* It was a comfort, or it would be, in time.

Ruth dropped Harmony and Molly to their new school just out of Cheltenham, and stayed long enough to make it clear to the head teacher and staff that the two girls had a duke's daughter standing behind them and taking a personal interest in their well-being. She then left for Winds' Gate, anxious to talk to her father about some changes she was determined to make.

She had agreed to the trip to the Midlands out of restlessness— a formless but vast dissatisfaction with the parameters of her life. She had blamed the bigotry and arrogance of English Society, which demanded that she complied with their every silly rule and ritual, but sneered down their collective noses at her anyway.

Two months at Ashcroft Hall had convinced her that she needed to shoulder some of the blame. She'd let the English define how she should behave, but why should she? As a duke's daughter, she outranked most of them. She'd had months of using her skills and being praised and respected for them, and she wasn't going back.

Something Drew had said had given her a different perspective on the rare occasions she'd forgotten her quest to be more English than the English, and had shared her medical knowledge with those who needed it. She'd focused on the loud chorus of detractors, but it was true that she'd won the admiration and friendship of the Prince Regent when she gave him an infusion of hashish oil to rub on his gouty feet. Indeed, that had led to consultations with others of the Royal Family, including the Queen Dowager, who was now taking a tisane of ginger and peppermint each day to help her sleep. And the Royals were only some of her admirers.

She wasn't going to try to fit in any longer. So what, if many in Society despised her as foreign and different? If they regarded her as a failure because she was twenty-four and unwed? Why should she care about the opinions of people she didn't even like?

The first hours in the main country residence of the duchy disappeared quickly. Warm greetings from those of the family in residence were followed by exchanges of news about those not currently at home. It wasn't until after dinner that she could have the private moment she requested from her father. "My study, Ruthling?" he suggested. She nodded, determined to say her piece while the words she'd rehearsed during the journey were still clear in her head.

"Kaka," she began, addressing her father with the Turkmen equivalent of the English 'Papa', "Rosemary tells me you plan to go from here to London and then on to Brighton."

"Yes, my dear. Will you come? We're all going to London, since we're expecting John." John, the duke's third son, kept a house in Egypt but was usually at sea, as he was in charge of the family's shipping business. "London will be quiet at this time of year, but half the Polite World will be in Brighton. I know you find the *ton* difficult."

Ruth accepted the perfect opening. "Some of them, Kaka. Not all. The noisiest ones, perhaps. I intend to ignore them from now on, if it will not embarrass you, or cause problems for Rosemary and my cousins."

Winshire's warm smile lit his eyes. "Your cousins go their own way, and so does Rosemary. Be yourself, Ruthling, and let the gossips flap their lips as much as they like. I trust you to be a lady as your mother was, and the twittering of jealous females with empty heads and too much time will not change that."

Ruth let out a breath she hadn't known she was holding. "I won't ride astride in Hyde Park, but I will stop making a secret of my craft as a physician. I won't abjure all social occasions, but I will refuse invitations or accept them as it pleases me. I won't go out of my way to insult those who whisper about me, but I will answer any cuts or slights with my own scorn. Will this displease you, Kaka?"

"It will please me very much, my daughter." One corner of his mouth quirked. "I would like to watch."

Ruth chuckled. "In that case, I should come with you to Brighton. And I will certainly come to London. I have in mind to set up a clinic for poor women and their children; somewhere they can have their illnesses and injuries treated without fear, paying only what they can afford."

"An excellent venture," the duke agreed. "Talk to Sophia. Your sister-in-law has much experience in such charitable enterprises. Your cousins, too. Sarah, as you know, helps women who need to escape violent men, and Charlotte runs a ragged school for slum children. They may have some ideas for you."

Sophia had already left Cheltenham for her home in Oxfordshire before Ruth got there, and the twins and their mother were visiting friends, but Ruth would certainly take her father's advice and consult them as soon as possible. She'd known about Sophia's interests in orphans and in education, but how had she missed her cousins' charitable ventures?

She and her father continued to talk about a possible place for the clinic, how Ruth might set it up, and the staffing she might need. She went up to bed humming with ideas. Tired as she was from her travel, she dropped quickly to sleep, but she woke in the night thinking of Val, remembering their kiss. She would not have minded another.

She got up to make herself a hot drink. This wakefulness had bedevilled her every night since they left Ashcroft Hall, and lying in bed would only lead to more musing about that kiss, and whether it had meant as much to Val as it did to her. He'd not given any indication that he wanted another; that he regretted losing her company. Did she mean more to him than a chance-met forced associate in the care of the patients he hadn't asked to be obliged to house?

She could and did argue both ways in the early hours of each morning. She repeated the reasons for the distance he set before them: Drew's arrival, Val's commitment to his girls, the English social rules that said a man and an unrelated woman could not correspond. She countered those reasons with the conviction that he would have found a way to court her if he were truly interested.

In the darkness before dawn, she faced the truth. Her determination to take life by the scruff of the neck and shake it into submission had less to do with giving up on something as trivial as social acceptance, and more to do with filling the void left by Val. No, not just the earl. Val, his daughter, and his niece.

14

———

L*eicestershire, July 1813*

The first letter from Ruth must have been sent a few days after she left Ashcroft Hall. It was, of course, addressed to the Ladies Mirabelle and Genevieve Monforte, so Crick delivered it to the schoolroom, which the girls now shared with the cook's children. Val, returning an hour later from the home farm, where he was helping bring in the second cut of hay, ran straight up to the schoolroom without taking time to change from his work clothes.

The girls greeted him with their usual exuberant hugs, and then wrinkled their noses. "Uncle Val, you smell dusty," Genny complained.

Val started to stand from the crouch that allowed the girls their hug. "I beg your pardon, my ladies. I shall wash and come back."

But small hands tugged him back into place. "It isn't a bad smell, Papa," Mirrie assured him. "Papa, we got a letter from Lady Ruth!"

"And Lord Andrew sent us each a ribbon for our hair," Genny added.

They tumbled over each other, both keen to share the news.

"And Harmony and Molly have started their new school. Lady Ruth says it is pretty, and the teachers seem nice."

"And Lady Ruth is going to write again from Winds' Gate."

"She hopes you are well, Papa, and Minnich and Crick and Nanny Pansy."

"She wants to hear how we are enjoying our new schoolroom."

"She hasn't got our letters yet, because she doesn't mention our new ponies, or your pictures of us writing her letters."

"She would, wouldn't she, Uncle Val? If she had got our letters?"

Val reminded the girls that they'd addressed their letters to Winds' Gate, then that he'd returned early to take them for their lesson on the quiet little ponies the stable master had found for their first experience as riders. "I will wash and change, and meet you at the stables in thirty minutes," he promised.

That very afternoon, after the riding lesson, the girls began their next letters to Lady Ruth, full of pony news. When they made their fair copy the next day, Val illustrated the bottom of each, under the signatures, with a fat little pony being ridden by with a tiny girl, legs stuck straight out the side, bouncing on its back.

Sure enough, the next letter from Ruth commented on the portraits of the girls—cartoons, rather, Val would call them. She wrote once a week, and the girls replied once a week, the letters crossing in the mail and, at Ruth's end, delayed when they had to be sent after her, as she travelled from Winds' Gate back to Cheltenham, on to Sutton Hall in Oxfordshire, to visit her brother and his wife, then to London and several weeks later to Brighton, where her family had rented a house for the summer.

"I would love to see the ocean," Mirrie sighed, and Genny suggested, "We could pretend the lake is an ocean."

"Oceans are much bigger, are they not, Papa? You cannot even see from one side to the other."

"You haven't seen an ocean," Genny objected. Genny usually followed Mirrie's lead, but as she became more confident and settled, she more and more often stuck up for her own opinion. Val agreed with Nanny Pansy that their occasional bickering was a good sign. Nevertheless, he opened his mouth to stop a disagreement before it began.

But Mirrie had the last word before he could intervene. "Crick has been on an ocean with Papa. The ocean is 'normous." She spread her arms as wide as she could, drawing out the syllables. "Isn't it, Papa?"

Val drew them on to his lap and told them stories of journeys he'd made by sea. The times he spent each day with his girls were the highlights of his day, and the three years before they came home seemed as distant as a nightmare dispelled by daylight. Even when he was with Genny and Mirrie, though, something was missing, and if he could ignore it in the day, when he was with the girls or busy about the work of the estate, the loneliness of night brought clarity.

Ruth was more than just the only friend of his own class he'd had since he left the army; she was the only woman friend he'd ever had. She was his heart's desire, his other half.

His problem was that he didn't know what to do about it. He had no idea how she felt about him. She could do better than him, that was obvious to the blindest of fools. But did she wish to?

Increasingly, as his yearning and loneliness grew in equal measures, he wanted to take the chance and ask her.

15

L*ondon*

Elspeth Ashbury entered the carriage in the mews behind her townhouse, her lover at her heels. It was deceptive; scruffy and rundown in appearance, but well-sprung and well maintained. The horses, too, were poorly groomed and mismatched, with a conformation that leaned more to cart horse than carriage horse. But they were powerful and well-trained, and could maintain a fast gallop for ten minutes or more through narrow streets while harnessed to the carriage.

Winderfield gasped at the luxurious appointments within the unprepossessing door. Elspeth, who had been collected by the same carriage several times in the past eighteen months, took a well-cushioned seat facing the direction of travel and opened the cupboard in the wall that contained brandy and glasses. "Drink, Windy?" she asked.

She wouldn't let Windy know, but she was annoyed to be summoned with no more than half an hour's notice. Stanley didn't care what plans of hers he disrupted. He expected to just snap his fingers and everyone would jump to obey.

Windy accepted the glass she offered him, but he shifted restlessly on the rear-facing seat, lifting the window curtain to peer out into the street. "Where are we going, Elspeth? I don't understand. I thought we were expected at the Sharps for dinner and then Lady Morpeth's soiree, and afterwards, a late appearance at the Opera. But this…" He spread a hand and gestured to the opulent interior of the coach. "What is happening?"

"I have sent a note to the Sharps," Elspeth deigned to explain. If she didn't answer the pest, he would whine like a baby. "You are very lucky, Windy. You are going to be presented to the Duke of Devil's Kitchen. Very few people have that privilege."

"Devil's Kitchen? The criminal?" Windy's eyes widened, and his restless shifting accelerated. "Why? What do we have to do with people like that?"

Could he be trusted with her secret? Probably not. His loyalty would evaporate like morning mist as soon as he saw a personal advantage in sharing any information she disclosed, and besides, he was stupid. He'd not understand the long-term benefits of keeping the Duke's real identity private.

Half a truth would do instead. "The Duke is the enemy of your uncle and his children, Windy, or had you forgotten that? He is our friend, and he offers his help."

"I do not have criminals for friends," Windy grumbled, conveniently forgetting his own attempts to murder his cousin. He continued to grumble, and Elspeth stopped listening, instead speculating on what might have prompted the Duke's summons.

Perhaps he had news for her? He had promised to dig up whatever information he could find to her brother-in-law's discredit. The Winderfield bitch, too, though Windy's sources and her own should have uncovered anything that was public knowledge. The third daughter of the Duke of Winshire was an insipid creature who apparently lacked the intelligence to know when she was being slighted, since she ignored the insults that regularly came her way.

The only notable thing about her was that she claimed to be a doctor. Apart from that, and her suspect birth and upbringing, Society's gossips did not have much to say, though Windy and Elspeth were changing that. Elspeth's lips curved upwards. Even the man they were about to visit acknowledged Elspeth's ability to manipulate the *ton's* scandalmongers was second to none.

The carriage stopped. From here, the streets were too narrow for the vehicle, but Stanley would have sent some of his toughs to escort them the rest of the way. Elspeth ignored Windy's spluttering about the possible damage to his shoes from the noxious state of the alley, and allowed one of Stanley's minions to assist her from the carriage. She headed down the narrow pathway between buildings, anxious to be inside where the crime lord had reproduced the luxury to which she had become accustomed since marrying Ashbury. Whatever his faults, the man knew how to make money. His recluse brother had the same gift, and was an improvement on her former husband in that he didn't stop Elspeth from spending it.

Windy would follow. If he did not come willingly, one of Stanley's men would drag him. Elspeth didn't look back to see. She had been asked to present him to the Duke of Devil's Kitchen, and that was what she would do.

16

———

L *ondon*

The reunion with John Winderfield was rapturous. He had even brought his wife, Zarina, and their three children, which was unexpected. Jamie proudly introduced Sophia, his wife, and she and Zarina were soon comparing notes on pregnancy, something Ruth knew a little about from a medical standpoint, but that otherwise left Ruth and Rosemary out of the conversation.

Two days of the men conducting business and the married woman discussing babies and children, then apologizing when they realized, yet again, that they were excluding Ruth and Rosemary, left the sisters anxious to find something to do, and Ruth knew just the thing.

Sophia had suggested a clinic near the ragged school that cousin Charlotte supported, which was at the less salubrious end of a long street, with merchant and trade households at one end and rooming houses of decreasing gentility at the other. One of the duke's agents had discovered two or three buildings that might be suitable for rental. Ruth decided she might as well make a start on inspecting them. "Will you come with me, Rosemary?" she asked her younger sister.

When they'd seen all three, Ruth thanked the agent and assured him she would consider all three buildings and let him know whether she wished to proceed with one of them.

"It is the warehouse, isn't it?" Rosemary asked, as they rode home in the carriage. "I was not impressed at first, but I can see the potential now that you have pointed it out to me."

Ruth's preference had previously been a storage building of some kind, in a side street full of small manufactories and warehouses. "It will need repair, some changes to walls and the like, painting and appropriate furniture, but I can see it working. Being away from residences might help, too. Hospitals can be noisy places. And there is space upstairs that could be made over into an apartment where a physician or surgeon could live, and manage the place." Ruth bounced in place, grinning broadly.

"I will need to have a builder look at it and see if my plans are feasible, but yes. I think that's the place."

Rosemary, the gentlest of her sisters and the only one anybody would describe as sweet, enthused with her as she babbled happily about all that needed to be done, writing reminders in the notebook she had brought for the purpose. "Here I am, talking on and on, and you without any interest in the clinic," she said at last, as the carriage made its way through the wide leafy streets beyond London proper, and turned into the square that had grown up in front of the town mansion of the Winshires.

"Not at all, Ruth. It was fascinating and I am glad I came."

Ruth found that hard to believe, but she gave her sister's hand a squeeze.

Rosemary chuckled. "It is true, dearest. I have no great enthusiasms myself, but I am drawn to those of others. I could listen to John talk about the sea for hours, and James on the topic of horses. You are the same when you start to talk about medicine. I envy you all, you know. I have no talents to speak of, and my interests are small domestic things."

How surprising! Her little sister, the perfect hostess and friend to everyone envied Ruth? "No talents?" She protested. "What of your gift for putting others at ease? And the way you always know the perfect thing to say, instead of staying silent or speaking far too much about things in which the company has no interest."

Rosemary waved off the remark. "That is not a talent. It is just that I find people interesting."

"Which is more than I do," Ruth acknowledged. "Most of them, anyway."

"Unless they have a broken leg or interesting spots," Rosemary teased, and they were laughing when they descended from the carriage to find their father and brothers watching them from the top of the mansion's steps.

"A successful excursion, I hope," the duke said, and Ruth soon found herself inside with a cup of coffee in hand, explaining her plans once again.

John's sojourn in London was quickly drawing to an end. Most of her time needed to be spent with him, his wife, and their children, for who knew when, or even whether, they would meet again in this life? Perhaps Ruth would travel one day to Alexandria in Egypt, where John and Zarina made their home when they were ashore, or even overland through the Levant or the lands south of Russia to the Caucasian kingdom ruled by her sister's husband and the mountains where her second brother was khan of Para Daisa and her eldest sister was wife to its sederke, its military commander.

London was empty of all but those who lived there year-round, but invitations still poured into the house from those who hoped to tempt a duke or a duke's offspring to grace their entertainments. By mutual consent, they sent polite apologies to all of them, instead enjoying their brief time together as a family. They did spend one evening at the Opera, crowding the duke's private box. The brothers took the children to admire the Tower of London and to Astley's Amphitheatre to watch the horses and acrobats. And they went *en masse* to the docks to tour the small merchant fleet—three sleek ships—that had brought John and Zarina to England.

Ruth managed to find time to commission a builder to inspect the property and to sign the purchase papers after receiving his estimate of costs for her changes and improvements. With the project underway, she could happily spend the rest of the summer in Brighton, with perhaps occasional trips to check progress. By winter, her clinic should be open for business.

Because they were not socialising, Ruth didn't notice people acting in a peculiar fashion until Rosemary pointed it out to her. "I wonder what the problem is," she commented, as they rode home one morning from an early outing to Hyde Park. "Three times today, people coming towards us turned aside onto a different path. I didn't say anything yesterday, when we took our niece and nephews to play in the square, but Mrs Wilmington collected her children and left, and so did two nursemaids with their charges."

"You think they were avoiding us?" That had been the norm for a few months during the worst of last year's feud with the Duke of Haverford, when he was challenging their legitimacy in a complaint to the Committee for Privileges. But their father's evidence had swung the Committee their way, and most people in Society now accepted them.

Rosemary frowned. "I thought they might be avoiding Zarina's children, but she and the little ones are not with us today."

After that, Ruth watched, and soon concluded something was going on. No one was overtly rude, but very few people directly approached them, and a number went to some lengths to avoid a casual meeting. Either that, or most of the people they came across while out walking were afflicted with a sudden need to cross the street or leave when the Winderfield family came into sight.

Or, more specifically, when Ruth appeared. Her brothers mentioned conversations that left no doubt that they were being treated as normal, and Sophia and Rosemary both had encounters with friends when Ruth was not with them.

It came to a head in Brown's Emporium, where the ladies of the family had taken Zarina to purchase English cotton and lace, and perhaps an English porcelain tea set. Ruth had grown bored with discussing the relative merits of shawls, and had wandered over to some rolls of heavy fabric that might do for curtaining in the physician's apartment.

The others were within earshot, so she heard when a lady addressed Sophia. "Lady Sutton! I had no idea you were in London."

"Lady Ashbury."

The name captured Ruth's attention, and she turned to watch. From the tip of her fashionable hat to her dainty leather-shod feet, the lady was an exquisite doll: the epitome of the English fashionable beauty, fair-haired, pale-skinned and blue-eyed. So, this was Val's sister-in-law?

Ruth stepped closer. The illusion of youth evaporated under closer examinations. Fine lines in the corners of the eyes, around the mouth, spoke of temper and a sour disposition, and those clear eyes were hard as she accepted an introduction to Rosemary and Zarina with a condescending nod.

Sophia turned to hold out her hand to Ruth, beckoning her closer. "And this is my sister Lady Ruth," she said. "Ruth, Lady Ashbury is related to…"

In one sweep of her eyes, Lady Ashbury had examined Ruth from head to toe, sniffed, and turned her back. "Lady Sutton, I advise you to distance yourself from this female." She pitched her voice to be heard throughout the cavernous building. "She may have hoped to keep secret her dalliance with my monstrous brother-in-law, but the people near his lands were rightfully scandalised, and have taken steps to ensure the truth is known."

Sophia, bless her, showed no reaction to the accusation beyond raised eyebrows, and spoke so that the riveted onlookers could hear her reply. "Have you been spreading lying gossip again, Lady Ashbury? My sister was fully chaperoned at all times while nursing *your daughter* through smallpox. She has the full support of His Grace my father-in-law and all of her family and friends."

She then turned to the rest of their party. "Ladies, let us come back another time. I find the company here today… malodorous, and I owe you an apology for condescending to make the introduction."

Ruth was swept along in Sophia's wake, but looked back as they exited the warehouse. Lady Ashbury remained where they'd left her, staring after them with narrowed eyes. Several of the other customers were already converging on her. This was not over.

When they were safely back in the carriage, Rosemary wanted to accost every person who had snubbed Ruth in the past three days to disabuse them of their error, and even Ruth thought she should tell her father about the lies. Sophia, though, counselled her to wait. "The men will want to fix everything, but this kind of attack—and believe me, it is an attack—will not be countered by a frontal assault. We need to marshal our friends and make sure they know the truth, and Ruth, you need to be seen going about your day with the same grace and reserve you usually show.”

“Kaka will hear,” Rosemary warned. “There is never any use in keeping anything from him.”

That was true. Ruth, though, saw Sophia’s point. Her brothers wouldn’t take this well, and nor would her guard, who would consider their own honour challenged. She didn’t want their last few days with John’s family to be shadowed by their reaction to the rumours.

Sophia was thinking along the same lines. She offered a warm smile to Zarina. “We have two or three more days in London to enjoy our family reunion. After that, perhaps on the way to Brighton, we can tell the menfolk and decide a strategy.”

“What of this brother the woman mentioned?” Zarina asked. “Is he truly a monster, as she says?”

“Not at all!” Ruth blurted. “He is a fine man. That evil witch is trying to hurt him. None of it is true! Not a word.”

“Of course not,” Sophia soothed. “You had Zyba and the rest of the guard with you the whole time, and you were quarantined with your patients.” She explained to Zarina, “Ruth was nursing Lord Ashbury’s daughters through the smallpox, which is why she was in his home.”

Zarina nodded thoughtfully. “And you admire this lord very much, Ruth, yes? Then the answer is simple. Let your father negotiate a marriage, and you shall defang that vicious cat.”

Ruth assured her sisters that such a measure was neither necessary nor something either party wanted, even as her heart fed her vignettes of a life with Val and his girls. She would rather retire from Society forever than force Val into a marriage he didn’t want. But how she wished he wanted it.

It was time. Val avoided the road in the hopes of making this trip unobserved. He took the well-remembered path from his garden into the woods and then along hedgerows and across a couple of streams by a plank bridge and stepping stones. He hadn't used this path in nearly a decade; not since he had escorted his new wife to the refuge she'd made out of the old watchtower on the borders of Ashbury land.

Perhaps no one used it now; certainly, it was becoming overgrown in places, and the plank bridge was so rickety that Val chose instead to take a flying leap across the stream it spanned. He landed well up the bank, grinning. When he was a boy, he and his friends had scorned to cross the easy way, and jumping the stream had been their regular practice. This had been a favourite route to their most treasured place.

He climbed the slight elevation ahead of him and rounded a scrubby patch of hedge, and there it was. The focus of a thousand boyhood games. The building in which he had last made love to his wife. The place she'd hanged herself.

The old watchtower had not changed in his lifetime, and someone had kept the weeds trimmed from around it. Apart from his heart thundering as if it would burst from his chest, he might have dropped in on any summer morning of his boyhood memories. Perhaps, if it had been a moist autumn day, like the one on which he and Isabelle had said their last farewells, he would not have been able to force his legs to carry him the last few paces.

The key would not turn, but he had come prepared with oil. A good soaking, and he managed to move the damnable thing, unlocking the heavy latch. It never used to be locked, but Barrow had secured it after they removed Isabelle's body. The latch gave way with a mighty screech, and the flock of crows that roosted on the roof lifted into the air with loud complaints.

Val paused again, the door opened just a crack. *You must do this.* He couldn't avoid the regrets that bedevilled him or elude the ghosts that haunted his dreams, but he could face his fears. He had to, for the sake of his girls. It was unacceptable that the head of the Monforte family was unable to visit the last remnant of the ancestral home of the Monfortes.

He pushed the door the rest of the way open and stepped inside before his reluctance disabled him entirely. Everything that reminded him of Isabelle had gone. He vaguely remembered Barrow telling him that some of the tenants had packed up her furnishings and other belongings. He'd never asked where they were, because he hadn't wanted to know. Stored with the contents of her room at the Hall, probably, for that, too, had been cleared by his protective servants one day during his convalescence.

Somewhere in the attics? Perhaps Mirrie might want something of her mother's in the years to come. Genny, too, for he rather thought he should tell his dear niece the truth when she was old enough. Certainly, before she saw her supposed mother again, for he wouldn't trust Elspeth not to tell the girl some twisted version of the facts just to spite him.

But that was a decision for another day. For now, he needed to examine the tower from top to bottom and put at least some of his fears to flight.

As he prowled from level to level, looking into each of the rooms, the past that pressed in on him was much kinder than he'd anticipated. He'd been Robin Hood, here, storming the Sheriff of Nottingham's keep. He'd been King Arthur, and this his castle; a privateer, the terror of the seas, and this his ship. The tenants' and servants' children had cheerfully followed wherever his imagination had led.

The bedframe was still in the top chamber, probably because it had been built in the room, and the only way to get it out would be in pieces. Val laid a hand on the rail. Perhaps Mirrie was conceived in this bed. She probably was. He and Isabelle had found this private space much more conducive to intimacy than the room they'd been given in the family wing, just a wall away from the earl.

For the first time since he returned to consciousness in the ruins of his life three years ago, Val thought of how sweet it had been to hold his young wife in his arms. He had failed her, and his guilt over that was not going to go away. But he would not fail her daughters. He would remember their mother with love, and he would share the stories the girls needed to feel part of that love.

Given what he'd done, he was blessed to have the girls, and he would strive to be worthy of them. He didn't deserve more.

17

*L*ondon
Windy thoroughly enjoyed Elspeth's report of her encounter with the Winderfield female. The Duke, when he sent for her, was less pleased. "I said subtle attacks, dear one," he admonished. "From what I am told, your attack had all the subtlety of a brick in a sock."

Elspeth, left standing before the throne the slum lord occupied, knew better than to answer, or even to let her resentment show. Instead, she dipped her head in a posture of submission, which had the other benefit of hiding her eyes.

Stanley would not countenance any show of rebellion. He never had, even when he was a child in the schoolroom, seven years her junior. His father would never hear a word against his heir, and Stanley's talent for revenge over any perceived slight intimidated everyone else in the household into compliance with his every wish. Given the minions he had at his command now, any sanctions he applied were likely to be far more damaging than nettles in her bed or the murder of a loved pet.

"What should I do, Your Grace?" she asked, schooling her voice to a neutral murmur.

"I am glad you asked me." Elspeth glanced up at the humour in his voice. He lounged on his throne, his eyes lit with amusement. "You need a holiday by the sea, dear Elspeth. Take your Winderfield pet and go to Brighton." He snapped his fingers, and one of the hulking brutes that always attended him stepped forward to hand her a cloth bag, heavy with coins.

"My treat," the Duke purred. "Enjoy yourself, my sweet."

"Of course," Elspeth agreed, "but what of the Winderfield chit?"

There was nothing benign in the Duke's smile. "You shall continue with your work, of course. But be subtle, dearest. Subtle. Lay your web of scandal, and wait for the fly to step into it." He sat forward all of a sudden, slamming his hands down on the arms of his chair. "She is going to Brighton, you silly bitch. Why else would I send you there?"

Their goals marched together. Elspeth had to keep reminding herself of that. She would have her revenge for the way Sophia Belvoir, now Lady Sutton, had slighted her at the Duchess of Haverford's house party the Christmas before last.

Elspeth had thought to ingratiate herself with the duchess by attacking James Winderfield, who was the son and heir of the Duke of Haverford's enemy. Sophia must have been having an affair with the heir even then, since she had to marry Winderfield quite suddenly a few days later. She spoke in his favour, and of course the duchess supported her goddaughter.

Elspeth had hoped that the marriage would put Sophia out of Eleanor Haverford's favour, and thus repair Elspeth's standing with the great lady, but the coolness lingered.

Whatever Her Grace's opinion, the Winderfields deserved to be cast out of Society. Disgusting mongrels. Her own family, the Whartons, had not held a title since one of their forebears backed the Stuarts rather than the Hanover interlopers. But her family could name their ancestors back to the Conquest, and the Whartons had been a great name in England long before the Monfortes left their native France and kissed enough royal posteriors to be rewarded with the Ashbury earldom in the very county the Whartons had ruled time out of mind.

She accepted her dismissal from the Duke's presence, and allowed her brother's lackeys to escort her to the waiting carriage. Brighton it would be, then. To prepare a welcome for Ashbury's lover. How delicious.

18

B*righton, August 1813*

The Winshire party lingered another week in London after John's ships sailed, before decamping to Brighton, where the duke had taken a house an easy stroll from the beach promenade.

The rumours had arrived before them. No one was openly rude to Ruth's face—but then, she was usually in the company of her powerful brother and sister-in-law, or her even more powerful father. Still, people detoured to avoid her, and conversations grew frantic when she came into view and ceased when she approached.

A soiree at the Marine Pavilion made a difference. The Prince Regent kept her on his arm and told everyone within earshot that she was not just the prettiest physician he had ever had, but the only one who had ever done him an ounce of good. He repeated the words in each new room, making his royal favour clear, and Ruth guessed that her father had told him of the rumours.

Fortunately, Ruth was not the type of female His Highness favoured, being slender and considerably younger than him. Even so, his ponderous gallantry and his inappropriate squeezes and pats to parts of her anatomy, even more than his loud advocacy, made the evening a trial.

But the following day, they had afternoon visitors for the first time since their arrival in Brighton, and several invitations were delivered, the most urgent ones with apologies that the Winshire contingent had unaccountably been left off the list.

Ruth was pleased for her sisters' sake to join the social round, and attending entertainments gave her the chance to begin to sound people out about support for her clinic, but her best times were spent with family, and in writing letters to the Monforte girls.

She made a story for them of her experiences at the Pavilion: a visit to the prince who was once known as Florizel. Long ago, when he was young and his people loved him.

The prince in the story was a lion, old and sad, with a wounded foot that would not heal. He was stuck in his palace, surrounded by feline courtiers who sought his favour and talked about him behind his back. In her story, the visitor he stood up for was a mouse—a lady among the mice, but a shy little rodent nonetheless—who brought him medicine for his foot despite her fear of the cats who filled his court. The cats would have eaten the mouse, she wrote, but the prince protected her.

She described the Pavilion, and wished she had Val's talent to draw it for the girls.

When she was done, she read it through again, smiling at the word pictures she had made. They would enjoy it, she thought.

The owner of the inn ushered the Duke of Winshire into the private parlour the Duchess of Haverford had rented for this meeting.

"Is this the gentleman, my lady?" His question was perfunctory, and the way he looked at Eleanor Haverford could best be described as a leer. She didn't bother to correct his form of address, but merely nodded her reply. "Thank you. That will be all."

The leer broadened. "There's a key in the lock, but you won't be disturbed. I've given orders."

The Duke of Winshire held the door open, and his frown must have penetrated the foolish man's thick skin, for the innkeeper left with no further comments. The duke shut and locked the door behind him, then faced Eleanor with a shrug and a smile. "Small-minded fool."

Now that they were alone, Eleanor lifted her veil. "James. It is good to see you." They had crossed paths at the Pavilion the previous evening, but she had been with Haverford, and even the mere nod she gave James in passing had fetched a fifteen-minute rant from her husband that ended only when the Prince Regent summoned him.

James bowed over her hand. "I am pleased to see you, my dear. You are looking well."

Her fingers tingled where he touched them, and she allowed herself the momentary indulgence of the wish that the innkeeper's assumptions were true. But she was a married woman and her honour would not allow her an affair. Not that James had ever hinted at desiring such a thing. He was still in love with his dead wife, and if he desired a bed partner, England abounded in younger and lovelier women than she, many of whom would be delighted to accommodate a handsome duke, with or without a ring on their finger.

"Shall we sit?" James prompted.

Eleanor shook off her thoughts, and took the chair by the tea tray she had ordered. Or should that be coffee and tea tray? James had returned from the East with a taste for thick black coffee, and she poured it for him just the way she had learned he liked it, then prepared her own cup of the gentler beverage.

As she carried out the ritual, they exchanged family news, while she wondered how to introduce the subject that had prompted her request for this meeting.

He gave her an opening when he mentioned his daughter Ruth. "She has been in quarantine in the north—a trip to a school that Sutton's wife sponsors turned into a battle with smallpox. I am pleased to have her back with family again."

"I had heard, James, and what I heard concerns me. Unkind gossip is insisting that she has been staying unchaperoned in the home of a widower with a fearsome reputation—a monster who killed his own wife and who is shunned by the entire county for his ravages amongst their women."

James could summon a fearsome scowl when he chose, but he had never before turned that ducal glare on her. "Lies!" He half rose from his seat with the force of his ire.

Eleanor had many years of remaining calm in the face of a far more threatening man than James. "Of course, and I am happy to play my part in saying so. But it would help to know what small modicum of truth the lies are built on, so I can more effectively demolish them."

James sat again, the ire dissipating as if she had poked a hole in the bubble that held it. "I beg your pardon, Eleanor. I thought asking the Prince Regent to lend her his countenance would help, and it did, for a few days." He swept his hand back over his hair, resting it for the moment on the crown, the picture of frustration.

"And now they are saying that she bribed him with her favours." Eleanor expelled her breath is a scornful huff. "Which is ridiculous. A less likely siren one could not wish to meet and, in any case, Prinny has always favoured motherly women of a certain age, not fresh young maidens. Besides, all of England is well aware that you, your sons, and your retainers would take offense at any insult to your ladies."

"Is that what they're saying?" James's face was grim, and Eleanor pitied anyone foolish enough to repeat the calumny within his hearing.

"They are, but I doubt if anyone actually believes it. If we deal with the supposed relationship between the Earl of Ashbury and your daughter, the rest will disappear. Now tell me all, James. Is Ashbury mad, as the rumours say?"

Ashbury Hall

Val surveyed the field with considerable satisfaction. "That's the last of it, Barrow." The Ashbury farms were more prosperous than they had ever been, and Val had expanded the investments his brother had begun. Both land and coffers were in good heart.

"Aye, my lord, and a good crop it is, too. We'll get another crop before winter, I'm thinking." Barrow must be as tired as Val, but he looked as solid and as reliable as ever.

Val clasped the man's hand. "Thank you, Barrow." Not just for the work today, but for the support he'd given this past three years. Respect, too, even when Val was a bumbling soldier with no idea how to get a crop in the ground or a harvest out of it. Trust most of all, as Val gained confidence and began to share the results of the extensive reading on land management he'd started as soon as he was well enough.

He couldn't say all that and embarrass them both. The handshake would have to do. Val said his farewells before he blurted something inappropriate, and set off across the fields. His pace quickened as the house came into view. What a difference the girls had made. Who would have thought two small females could have filled the dismal old manor with sunlight and laughter—penetrating Val's ossified heart until he couldn't imagine life without them. There they were! They must have been walking in the little home wood, for they were just crossing the lawn in front of the house.

"Girls!" Val called, and they abandoned their nursemaid to race towards him, Genny's slightly longer legs covering the ground faster so she reached him first, wrapping her arms around him, sure of her welcome. Mirrie was only a moment or two behind, her hug encompassing both cousin and father.

"I should run faster," she complained. "I am the eldest."

Val kissed the top of her head. "You are dainty, like your mother, my love. Genny, here, is of a statelier build, and so her legs are longer. She takes after the Monfortes."

"I would like to take after the Monfortes," Mirrie grumbled. She gave Genny another hug before taking Val's offered hand. "Genny always wins when we race."

Genny attached herself to Val's other side, wrapping her hand around his arm just below the elbow. "But you get to hide in the best places, Mirrie, because you are smaller than me."

Val smiled as they began to walk back towards the waiting maid, and the two girls continued to argue the relative merits of Mirrie's delicate frame and Genny's more sturdy build. Even in their frequent debates, each was protective of the other. How he loved them!

They went in through the front door. "Off upstairs and wash," Val told them, "and then we shall read in the library until dinnertime."

He really ought to see about a governess for them, but this summer holiday had done them no harm. They'd gained back the weight they'd lost when they were ill, and the time they spent outdoors had painted their formerly wan complexions with healthy roses.

"Letters, my lord," Anders, the new butler, said, and Genny turned back on the stairs, her face lighting with hope. Poor child. She wrote to Elspeth every week, but Mirrie had confided that Elspeth never wrote back, not even on birthdays or at Christmas.

To put her out of her misery, Val leafed quickly through the small stack of correspondence, setting aside a couple from his lawyer and one from the clever fellow who managed his investments. The remaining two had both been franked by the Duke of Winshire. Ruth? The handwriting was different on each. The one addressed to the two girls was from the lady. The hand on the one addressed to him was bolder. The duke himself? The frisson of guilt was silly. The man couldn't possibly be aware of Val's erotic dreams, or even of the amazing kiss he and Ruth had exchanged in real life.

"Girls, I have a letter from Lady Ruth for the pair of you. You may have it when you join me downstairs." He reluctantly put it back on the salver, keeping hold of the other, before following the girls upstairs for his own wash.

He opened the letter, looking at the signature first, while Crick buttoned him into his clean shirt and put his feet into a pair of indoor shoes. Not the duke. Drew W. Lord Andrew Winderfield then, Lady Ruth's brother. He read through, surging to his feet so quickly that Crick fell backwards. "My lord," the valet protested.

Val returned to his seat, but though he held his body still, but for presenting his wrists for the cuff buttons, and his neck for his cravat, his mind continued in ferment. Lord Andrew wrote of the latest scandal seething through the *beau monde*, and Val was its object. Val lifted the letter so he could read the salient points again, while Crick fussed over his cravat.

"*…your injuries have driven you mad, so that you are as much a monster within as you appear without…*" No mealy-mouthed skirting around the point, there. Were all the Winderfields as direct?

"*…you killed your brother and your wife, and your brother's wife escaped by inches, having first hidden the children away for their own safety…*" Which was no more than had been spoken in the village before they grew to know him again, though at least they knew that Val's brother was dead and buried before he arrived home, too sick to be a threat to anyone.

"*… even the local villagers shun you, knowing of your madness…*" Also true, or at least, it used to be.

The gossip wasn't just about him, however.

"*… would have warned you anyway, but this gossip also touches my sister's honour. The common thread in the rumours about her is that you lived together for weeks. Some say you abducted her. Some say she came willingly. Either way —or so the rumours claim—you ruined her and cast her off when you had sated your lust.*"

Drew seemed more amused than indignant when he wrote, "*Those who believe that Ruth and her guards would allow such a thing don't know our family very well. But they shall know us better, I warrant you.*"

Winshire had ordered an investigation into the source of the gossip. Once Crick had placed his cravat pin, Val reached for the third page, which he read several times before allowing Crick to help him into his coat.

"*My sister-in-law suspects the Countess of Ashbury, your brother's widow. From our encounter when I was with you, Lady Harwood may be providing local detail.*" Undoubtedly. Others too, probably.

Even without what they were saying about Ruth, Val would need to squash this nonsense for the sake of his girls. But the lies and half-lies about Ruth required immediate action.

"Crick, tell Minnich that I want to see you and her in my study as soon as the girls go up to bed." The first step was to find the traitors under his own roof. Then he'd have another word with Sir William Harwood about muzzling his wife—the man had already made some overtures as Val took on more and more responsibilities in the community. He'd even made an apology of sorts.

Then Val would take on Society. Just a couple of months ago, he would have quailed at the thought of venturing to Brighton and even London. Now, any apprehension was swamped in the feelings that had him smile as he shrugged into the coat that Crick held ready. In a matter of days, perhaps a little over a week, he would see Ruth again.

19

———

B*righton*

The respite in the gossip lasted only a week. "Someone is stirring the scandal broth," Sophia surmised. They didn't have to name the source. They all knew it was Lady Ashbury. They saw the nasty woman everywhere, and it was no surprise to find her in attendance the night they went to the opera.

The family went as a treat for Rosemary, who had been enthralled with opera since her first attendance. "England offers a few compensations for what we have given up to come here," she declared, "and opera is one of them." Many of the audience had other motivations to be there: to see and be seen, to ogle the dancers, to gossip and socialise. Rosemary went for the performance, and the lead singers tonight were among her favourites.

The high level of interest in the box Jamie had leased for the Brighton season may have had nothing to do with Lady Ashbury. Coincidences happened, of course, but Ruth didn't believe this was one.

"Do you see who the Ashbury woman is with?" Sophia whispered under the cover of her fan. Ruth peered while trying to look as if she had no interested in Lady Ashbury and her party. Sure enough, someone sat in the shadows behind Lady Ashbury's seat.

Ruth couldn't make out more than a general outline. Jamie, who was sitting behind his wife, leaned forward to murmur, "It's the Weasel. I saw him when I went to fetch your drinks during the interval."

Weasel was a Winderfield cousin—a distant cousin who had believed himself to be heir presumptive to the dying Duke of Winshire, Ruth's grandfather, when the Polite World thought Ruth's father long since dead. He had not taken his displacement well, even going to the length of hiring assassins.

"I wonder what his relationship is with Lady Ashbury?" Sophia mused. "I hear he is seen everywhere with her."

"I wonder where he is living," Jamie growled. "It seems he needs a visit to remind him of the terms of his release." The Winderfields had kept Weasel an enforced guest at Winds' Gate until the Committee of Privileges had ruled on the legitimacy of the duke's children, and released him under threat of prosecution if he ever threatened any of the family again.

His volume had crept up, and Rosemary hissed a 'shush' without taking her eyes off the stage. Jamie sat back, but Ruth knew he and Sophia wouldn't let the matter end there. An 'I wonder' from either of the Suttons was a declaration of intent. Within a day or two, they would have their answers.

Indeed, when she walked along the path above the beach the following day, Sophia went from group to group, greeting ladies of her acquaintance and carefully guiding the conversation to their disreputable cousin. Jamie must have done something similar in the places the gentlemen gathered, because both of them were able to report by the time the family gathered before dinner.

"Weasel Winderfield is living in the townhouse Lady Ashbury has taken for the summer," Jamie reported.

The duke raised his eyebrows. "A toxic combination. How long has that been going on?"

Sophia had the answer. "At least six months. In London, he is her guest, too. Hostesses who invite Lady Ashbury anywhere know to include Mr Winderfield in the invitation."

The duke looked from Jamie to Drew. "I can depend on the two of you to suggest to young Weasel that he remember the terms of his release, unless he is in the mood for a long, one-way sea voyage, with plenty of healthy exercise?"

That had been the other alternative to prosecution: being handed over to John to use as a sailor. Not that the soft landlubber would be much use on a ship.

"What of Lady Ashbury?" Sophia asked. "A pity Aunt Georgie and Aunt Grace are not here." The duke's sister and sister-in-law were formidable Society leaders. "Shall I have a word with her?"

The duke smiled. "It is in hand, my dear. Her Grace of Haverford will deal with it."

The widow was not one of Eleanor Haverford's usual circle. She was too young to be one of the titled ladies with whom the duchess had ruled Society for more than thirty years, and too old to be one of their daughters.

That was not the real reason Eleanor barely knew her, of course, as Eleanor admitted to herself. The real reason was that Eleanor liked cats only when they had whiskers and four paws. Lady Ashbury was a cat of the human kind: one for whom the less influential members of Society were mice to hunt and torment.

If an innocent action could be given a vicious interpretation, Lady Ashbury would find it and the sycophants who clustered around her would spread it. And woe betide the person, lady or gentleman, who made a misstep in negotiating the silly rules that governed the lives of the *ton*. It would be magnified a thousandfold if Eleanor and her own allies were not in time to mitigate the damage.

Lady Ashbury sat in Eleanor's formal drawing room, a striking beauty still, though she was in her late thirties. She should look colourless in her light blue walking dress and white spencer, with white-blonde hair drawn into fashionable ringlets that did not dare to do anything so indecorous as bounce, delicately darkened brows arching over ice-blue eyes. Instead, in the sumptuous splendour of the room, she drew the eye, like a diamond centrepiece that outshone the splendour of an ornate collar of gold and gems.

"How kind of you to invite me, Your Grace," she purred. "I have long wished to be better acquainted. I admire you so much, and feel for you. I understand what it is like to be married to a man who is persistently unfaithful. My husband, too…" She trailed off.

Eleanor smiled, a baring of teeth containing little amusement. If this upstart thought the Duchess of Haverford was going to be manipulated to play her game of insinuation and scandal, she could think again.

"You were invited for one reason only, Lady Ashbury. I understand you are taking some notice of Lady Ruth Winderfield, the daughter of the Duke of Winshire."

Lady Ashbury dropped her lashes to veil her eyes. "You have an interest in the matter, of course. The feud between Winshire and Haverford is well known to me, Your Grace."

Eleanor allowed none of her disgust to show. "Your motivation, of course, is your brother-in-law, whose name you have chosen to couple with that of Lady Ruth."

The woman looked up, a flash of spite in her eyes. "They connected their own names, Your Grace, when she stayed with him, unchaperoned."

Eleanor could argue that Ruth had her companion with her, as well as a bevy of armed retainers, a maid, and six children; that she was taking refuge during a smallpox epidemic; that she was providing medical care for several people, including Lady Ashbury's own daughter. But Lady Ashbury was not interested in facts, but in fixing her claws into the weak. This time, she had chosen the wrong targets.

Eleanor showed her own claws. "I would take it amiss, Lady Ashbury, if these rumours continue to circulate. Very amiss."

An expression at last. Alarm, quickly concealed. Lady Ashbury's tinkling laugh was unamused. "You jest, duchess. Haverford hates the chit's father."

Eleanor raised a brow. "I have not invited you to address me as an intimate, young woman. Nor will I."

Colour flooded Lady Ashbury's face. "Your Grace. My apologies, Your Grace."

"You have miscalculated, Lady Ashbury. His Grace of Haverford cannot abide scandal-mongering women." A slight exaggeration, but his pride, which would see an insult to his wife as an insult to him, would ensure that he supported Eleanor, at least in public, which was all that mattered.

"In addition, I am dearest friends with Lady Ruth's aunt. I must thank you, however, for drawing my attention to the Earl of Ashbury. I had not noticed his absence from society since his brother's death. I intend to amend that oversight. Your brother-in-law shall be presented to the Regent under my sponsorship and that of His Grace, the Duke of Haverford. I suggest you make yourself least in sight for the remainder of the little season. A sojourn in the country might be good for your health, Lady Ashbury."

Lady Ashbury sat, as pale as her spencer, her mouth open.

Her Grace stood and pulled the bell chain. "My footman shall show you out," she said.

Travelling with children had Val joking with Crick that this journey compared unfavourably with some of the forced treks they'd completed in rain and mud, and under fire. Each day's travel began once the girls were up and breakfasted, was interrupted regularly for food and comfort stops, and, as Nanny Pansy put it, "So the young ladies can stretch their legs." And by five in the afternoon, they had either arrived at a suitable inn or were looking for one with increasing anxiety, so that Genny and Mirrie could be fed, bathed, and put to bed. "They will have trouble sleeping in a strange bed, my lord," Nanny Pansy assured him, "but better a long-disturbed night than a short one."

Val did what he could to help the nurse with the burden of two overwhelmed and over excited girls. He travelled for part of each day in the coach, playing games and making up stories about the scenes outside the windows. He accompanied the girls for a walk at each stop. He took each girl up before him on his horse for half an hour at a time, at least twice a day.

At last, they arrived in London. Val had calls to make and arrangements to set in progress before the final day of travel to

Brighton. Two or three nights in the same place wouldn't hurt the girls, either.

He took rooms at Grillions—a suite with a bedchamber for him and Crick and another for the girls and Nanny Pansy. In the morning, he sent them off to view some of London's sights: Hyde Park, the Tower of London, London Bridge. "Don't let them out of your sight," he instructed Crick and their young coachman, one of Fletcher's nephews, as he put them into a hire carriage.

Val went his own way. First stop was the Ashbury townhouse on Marshall Square. The knocker was off the door, but a solid knock, repeated several times, eventually fetched a response. The door opened a crack and the person behind it growled, "Nobody at home. The mistress is away."

Val nudged the door open enough to put his booted foot in the way of it shutting and replied, "But the master is here and requires entrance."

"The master is dead," the man grumbled, his voice no more welcoming.

"My brother is dead," Val corrected, "but I am very much alive." He pressed against the door, and resistance melted away.

The servant stood blinking in the light that streamed in through the door as Val stepped inside. Val had never seen him before. "What became of Hammond?" he asked. Hammond had been butler at the London townhouse throughout Val's childhood.

The servant shook his head. "I don't know any Hammond, my lord."

Val let it go. Time enough to find out exactly what damage Elspeth had done while Val was licking his wounds in the Midlands. "Lady Ashbury has already left for Brighton?" he asked. Only time would tell if he needed to do a complete purge of the current servants when he took the house over, but meanwhile, pretending to be familiar with Lady Ashbury's plans might win him some compliance.

The servant nodded, and made no objection when Val announced his intentions of inspecting the house. He didn't even insist on following Val around. "You're him. The man in the painting."

Val raised a brow. His brother had commissioned a wedding painting of him and Isabelle, Val in full regimentals, but he'd had no idea Elspeth had kept it. He didn't see it, either, as he walked through the house, noting the changes. The public rooms had recently been redone in the latest style, with a heavy application of chinoiserie. Val remembered seeing the bills back when he was sunk in his own misery.

He found no sign of private papers. He wanted something he could use as evidence to convince Elspeth to go quietly. He was within his rights, of course, to turn her out of his home; to insist that his only obligation was to provide the stipend she regularly overspent and the dower property at Ashbury Hall. But she had been in Society and he had been invisible. The future he was beginning to envisage might be made awkward if she convinced the *ton* he was the villain of the piece.

The countess's quarters were also newly refurbished. The evidence that they were shared with a man, at least occasionally, reposed on shelves and pegs in the dressing room—men's clothes and shaving gear. Both bedside tables were clearly in use, too, and, unless Elspeth had developed a taste for brandy and port, the decanters on one of the low chests were further proof.

He found no letters or diaries in the bedchamber, nor did the desk in the private sitting room yield anything of interest.

The other rooms had a neglected air. Val walked through them documenting spaces on the walls where paintings once hung, display cabinets with nothing on display, ornaments and vases he remembered from previous visits that could not be seen anywhere. Had Elspeth put them away or had she been selling them off?

The top floor, just under the attics, was still servants' quarters. He left their rooms alone. Still no painting of him and Isabelle.

It wasn't in the library-cum-study, either. At least that was what the room had been when Val was last here. Elspeth had removed all the books, replacing them with porcelain figures, ornate vases, and large display plates. The solid oak desk by the window had been replaced with a spindly little thing in cherrywood that looked too fragile to write on. It had sturdy drawers, though. Locked, all four of them.

Val was contemplating whether to break the locks when the servant reappeared at the door. "Maude says I should ask you if you want tea," he grumbled.

"Thank you, but no. Maude is?"

The man looked blank for a moment, then realised Val was asking what Maude was to the house. He became briefly garrulous. "Maude is the cook, my lord. Just me and Maude here, at the moment. Her ladyship took the rest to Brighton with her. Those that were left. Had a big to-do just before she left for Brighton, when Mr W. got a bit frisky with Madam's lady's maid. Her ladyship didn't like that, and she fired Werther, the maid. So, the butler, who was sweet on the maid, he up and left, too, and he got a new position straight away and took three of the footmen with him."

"And you are?" Val coaxed.

"Jake, my lord. I'm the man of all work, sir. Are you coming to stay, my lord? Only, Maude wants to know on account of she needs to buy some food in, and her ladyship didn't leave any money."

"Tell Maude—no, wait. I'll come and talk to her myself."

Val descended to the kitchens to explain to the cook and the surly Jake that he was merely visiting, but that he planned to take over the house from his sister-in-law, and that he would reward those who were loyal to him. He reinforced the message with a sovereign each. Bed and board were part of the arrangement between an employer and their house servants. For Elspeth to go away without leaving food money for these two was unconscionable, though not out of character.

Jake cheered up immensely, though whether at the sovereign or the news that Elspeth's tenure was nearly over, Val couldn't say. Maude offered him tea again, saying that she and Jake were about to have one. "Go ahead," Val answered. "I need to get back to my daughters, so I'll just let myself out, shall I?"

They let him go upstairs unaccompanied, and—after a moment's thought—he picked up the entire light desk and carried it off into the street, where he and the hire-carriage he hailed had the fun of trying to fit it through the narrow carriage doors. He found a locksmith who promised to have it open for him within thirty minutes, and to provide him with replacements for his 'lost keys'.

The next stop was his solicitors. It was time and past time to make sure that Elspeth could no longer draw on the earldom's accounts. She had her own generous settlements and a quarterly allowance, and he would expect her to live on those. "In addition, I shall provide a house in the place of her choosing," he told the solicitor. "This shall be in lieu of the dower property at Ashbury Hall." Because he didn't want Elspeth anywhere within reach of his family. "However, I shall no longer be responsible for her bills. She is drawing well over the allowance to which she is entitled as my brother's widow. Please write up a list of all merchants who send you their accounts. They'll need to be informed that Lady Ashbury will, in future, be paying her own bills."

The solicitor sucked his lips into his mouth. Val said, "Speak up, man. What is troubling you?"

"And the gambling debts, my lord? Will you be repudiating them, as well?"

"You've been paying her gambling debts?"

The solicitor sputtered something about an arrangement of long-standing, and Lady Ashbury's assurances that the earl had proposed it. Val was sure the man didn't believe that, but no doubt neither Elspeth nor the solicitor expected him to come to London and challenge her expenses.

He would probably need to find another solicitor. To be fair, he'd left the man without supervision, and Elspeth could be charming when she chose. Still, he'd picked up the reins of the earldom within a few weeks of leaving his sick bed and letters had passed between him and his solicitor ever since.

Furthermore, Val would have questioned any substantial amounts that were unexplained. The solicitor must have been hiding the gambling debts in some way, and who knew what other money had slid out of the accounts sight unseen?

Yes. Another solicitor. Perhaps Drew Winderfield might know of someone trustworthy.

The locksmith handed him a box with the contents of the desk drawers, and Val and his coachman manhandled the desk back into the carriage. Returning it to the townhouse was simple enough. His knock this time was answered quickly, and Jake greeted him with a bow, stepping aside so that Val could enter.

"Jake, you mentioned my wedding portrait. I didn't see it when I was here before. Can you show it to me?"

"Of course, my lord." He bowed again. The two hours he'd had to think about Val's visit had clearly made him a loyalist for the man who ultimately paid his wages. "Her ladyship wanted it taken down, my lord, and I'm the one who wrapped it and put it in the attic."

Excellent. A trip to the attic would work perfectly. "Lead on, Jake." Val closed the door without latching it, and followed Jake up the stairs. When he came back down twenty minutes later, his wedding portrait under his arm, he glanced into the study. The desk was back in front of the window.

It was time to re-join his family, but this evening he'd check the papers he'd purloined from Elspeth's desk. The visit to the attic had been fruitful, too. Not only had he retrieved the painting, but he'd established that the attic didn't contain enough boxes to account for all the missing items in the house. Elspeth had a lot to answer for.

20

B*righton*

Two days after her meeting with the Duchess of Haverford, Elspeth still hadn't decided whether to let Stanley know that Her Grace had decided to interfere. As she stepped out of the chair she had hired to bring her and Windy home from The Steyne, she was considering the wording of a judicious letter.

Stanley might not understand that she had no power to withstand an edict by the great lady. Windy agreed they had to stop their whispering campaign, though Elspeth took some satisfaction in knowing that it had taken on a life of its own in the hands of the gossips and scandalmongers, and even the combined influence of two ducal families would find it hard to eradicate the stain.

Ashbury would likely never find a female to marry him now, even if he did ever poke his head out from his own lands. Lady Ruth might manage a match. Her father was purportedly as wealthy as Midas, and could easily buy her some poverty-stricken peer who couldn't afford to turn his nose up at the stupid cow's dark skin and tarnished blood lines.

Her self-congratulation stuttered to a halt as she entered her hall to find it full of large rough men. Windy came to a halt at her back, and would have slithered back out the door, except that one of the bully boys put a large hand on it and closed it firmly.

The man she recognised as Bruno, one of Stanley's lieutenants, gestured with his thumb towards her drawing room. "His Nibs is in there. He wants to see you straight away."

Despite her bounding heart and sweaty palms, Elspeth kept her voice smooth and arrogant, as she lifted her chin and replied, "I shall just pop up and take off my pelisse."

One of the brutes moved to block the stairs, and Bruno repeated, "Straight away." Elspeth glared, and Bruno repeated, "Straight away." His voice took on a mocking tone as he bowed and gestured to the door one of his cohort held open, saying, "My lady."

She swept past him. Behind her, Windy muttered something about going to his room, and was told to sit and stay. There'd be no help from him.

Stanley sat at his ease on her favourite couch, sprawled out to take up most of the space. He had eschewed his favourite silken robes for the formal day wear of a gentleman, and did not look at all out of place, apart from the aura of menace that was as natural to him as breathing.

"My dear!" She would get in first, before he could explain what brought him. "How wonderful to see you! Have you come down from London just for me? I'm honoured."

Stanley didn't bother with niceties. "You told me that Ashbury was a crippled idiot, afraid of his own shadow, and incapable of leaving his own property. You were wrong. Ashbury will be here, in Brighton, today or tomorrow."

"Impossible! I would have heard!"

Stanley was uncompromising. "He has been in London, seeing his solicitor and taking back his house."

Elspeth sank into the nearest chair, her mind blank of anything but panic.

"If we do not destroy him, my dear Elspeth, you will be homeless and very likely penniless."

"I… but…"

Stanley smiled. "No need to worry. I have a plan. First, you are going to be reunited with your dear, dear daughter."

21

———

They accomplished the trip to Brighton in a day, but arrived too late for Val to go visiting. The rental property he'd written ahead for was outside of town. It was as comfortable as promised, though, and the staffing—a butler, two footmen, a cook and kitchen maid, and two housemaids—was more than adequate.

He put one of the footmen to use immediately, writing a message to be taken to the Winshire townhouse. To Drew. A single man could not write to an unmarried lady. He then went up to the little suite of rooms given over to the nursery party, to have tea with his girls and help put them to bed.

Perhaps arriving at his destination was to blame. Certainly, he had trouble falling to sleep, despite the tiredness due to travel, torn between his concern about the coming confrontation with Elspeth and the joy that he was only a few miles from Ruth and would probably see her the next day. At some point, he slipped into unconsciousness, only to find himself back in Spain, searching farm buildings for French snipers. He burst into one building, gun in one hand and sword in the other, to stop in shock at the sight of a girl, swinging by her neck from the roof beam. In the next moment, he was ambushed from behind the door, a sabre swinging down onto the hand with the gun. Even in the dream, he remembered that in real life, he had not stood there stupidly, watching the blood gush from his wrist. Indeed, he had swung his own sword, killing his assailant. And the Frenchman had not succeeded in severing his hand; that had been the action of a surgeon a week later, after an infection in the mangled fingers threatened his life.

Still, in the dream, he was frozen in shock, until the shadow of the girl moved over him, and he looked up to see it was his dead wife hanging in the tower room on his home estate. So far, the usual nightmare, but then, as she turned slowly, spinning on her rope, her features changed and it was Ruth, choking and gasping as she stran- gled, and Val unable to move, unable to use his useless arm to free her.

He woke, tangled in sweaty sheets, his heart racing and his breath catching on aching sobs of loss.

The miasma of the dream hung over him as he washed and dressed, had a cup of coffee—the only thing he wanted near his stomach—and read the note that Drew had sent this morning in response to his. His recovery began with Drew's invitation: "Come over as soon as you like. Bring the girls; Ruth is anxious to see them." The arrival of his girls, keen for a morning kiss, allowed him to brush the last remnants of remembered horror away. It was only a dream, and the last change, the unexpected one, was only because he was here in Brighton to see Ruth, to court her, if she would agree.

He took Drew's advice, and brought Genny and Mirrie as a buffer, and Nanny Pansy to look after them while he consulted in private with the adults. The horses were tired from the previous day's journey and would, in any case, have to be delivered to the post inn, and his carriage needed a good clean, so they went into town in a barouche hired that morning—another errand for the useful footman, who ran down to the livery stable before breakfast.

Drew waited until they were all gathered at breakfast to announce, "The Earl of Ashbury sent me a note last night, but I didn't see it until this morning."

Ruth looked up to find her brother's gaze upon her as he added, "He is in Brighton, and he and his young ladies will call this morning."

"Morning is early for a call," Sophia objected. Ruth was ready to argue, but Drew answered before she could.

"He is here to deal with his sister-in-law, Sophia, and wants to find out what we know before he calls on her. I wrote back to him before I came into breakfast, and told him to visit as soon as he liked and to bring the children." He grinned at Ruth. "I thought you would like to see them, Ruth."

Ruth nodded. Did she have time to change into something more fashionable? No! How silly. He wasn't coming to court her. He was coming to discuss strategy for dealing with Lady Ashbury. She looked well enough in the comfortable gown she had donned for a day at home.

"Ruth, you've put sugar in your tea," Rosemary whispered. Ruth flushed. She had not even been aware that she had a cup of tea in front of her.

She ignored her error and spoke to the table at large, with an assumption of calm. "It will be pleasant to see the children." From the amused looks cast her way, she was fooling no one, least of all herself.

Mercifully, no one commented on her mistake with the tea or her sudden loss of appetite, and she was soon able to slip away to the library to read her mail, which included letters from Charlotte and Sarah, her twin cousins, full of advice for raising funds for her clinic. There was also a report from the architect she had left in charge of the clinic work.

The letters might as well have been written in Sanskrit for the sense they made, as she started at every sound from beyond the library walls, straining her ears for signs that Val had arrived.

By the time he and the girls turned up in the late morning, she was a bundle of nerves, and thoroughly ashamed of herself for allowing her imagination to run away with her. Val had never said anything to indicate he wanted a closer relationship than friend. She had built a castle in the air on the foundation of one kiss and some warm looks, none of which came anywhere close to a declaration of intent.

A person did not need to be anxious about meeting a friend.

She took a moment to gather her dignity and paste calm over her inner turmoil, then stepped out of the library, to be greeted exuberantly by two excited little girls, who had to be hugged and admired and listened to before she could do more than sneak surreptitious glances at the man who watched the reunion with a beaming smile.

"These must be Lady Mirabelle and Lady Genevieve Monforte," the Duke of Winshire said, as he came down the stairs into the entrance hall.

Ruth disentangled the arms around her neck and stood to present the girls and Val to her father. "Your Grace, may I make known to you Lady Mirrie, Lady Genny, and Lord Ashbury."

The duke offered his hand to Val and smiled at the girls. "We have lemonade and cake in the drawing room. Might I escort you there, young ladies? My daughters are looking forward to making your acquaintance."

He took a hand each to lead them back up the stairs, trailed by Nanny Pansy.

Val offered Ruth his arm and one of the warm looks on which she had been refining far too much. She braced herself for the quiver as she gave him her hand, and sure enough, it trembled from that fortunate appendage all the way through to her core. *You are a sad case, Ruth Winderfield.*

Rosemary and Sophia were both already in the drawing room, charming the children and throwing speculative looks at Val. Ruth's brothers arrived at the same time as the tea trays, and Drew was greeted rapturously by the two Monforte girls, whom he then introduced to the other latecomers.

Val's girls were overcome with shyness. The adults, they had taken in their stride, but Ruth's youngest brother Thomas, just beginning to stretch into a string bean at thirteen years of age, had them retreating, one to Val, and the other to Ruth.

With rare tact, Thomas, beyond an initial polite greeting, ignored them, instead investigating the contents of the plates that cook had sent with enough food for an army of growing boys. Ruth would have thought the sandwiches and savoury tarts his only interest, except that he began a conversation with the next youngest brother, Barno, in a voice pitched to reach the girls, about the housekeeper's mouser, whose kittens had just reached the age of wandering the servant halls so that they had to be rescued and repeatedly returned to their mother.

Sophia, meanwhile, won Nanny Pansy's allegiance by serving her tea, refuting the nursemaid's embarrassed demurs by explaining that she remembered her own nursemaid as a treasured foundation of a happy childhood, and—now that she was herself with child—she would be making sure the person entrusted with that baby was treated with the respect that the important role deserved. "I am practising on you, Mrs Knowles," she said.

The little girls had so far recovered from their bashfulness by the time morning tea had been consumed that they accepted Thomas's invitation to meet the kittens as long as Nanny Pansy went too. Ruth sent a querying look at her father, who nodded, confirming that he'd enlisted the youngest Winderfield's support to remove the girls from the coming conversation.

As the door closed behind them, Val edged up to Drew. "When might we meet to discuss your letter?"

"Now would be an excellent time," Drew replied.

"What letter?" Ruth asked. Only Rosemary looked to Drew for an answer, and he didn't give it, instead grinning at Jamie. "I told you the letter would fetch him straight away."

Ruth turned to her father. "Kaka? What. Letter."

The duke was polite but uncompromising. "Ruthling, you insisted that Lord Ashbury was not to be bothered by this kerfuffle his brother's widow and our terminally stupid cousin have caused. But the matter touches on the man's honour. He had a right to know."

Even in her anger, Ruth could concede the point. But she hadn't wanted—still didn't want—Val riding hell for leather down to her rescue, and if he dared to propose to her under these circumstances, she would hit somebody. Even if she had spent all the weeks since their parting dreaming that he would follow her and ask her to marry him. But because he could not live without her, not because of a stupid rigmarole of lying gossip and the stupid rituals of the stupid English aristocracy.

"I should have been told," she insisted.

"Would you have come with us to Brighton if you had known?" Jamie could usually be depended on to see to fair play within the duke's brood, but even he, the traitor, justified keeping this secret from her.

Sophia looked nervous, and well she should. "We knew we'd have a better chance of scotching the rumours if you were seen in Society, and particularly if the Prince Regent made it clear he favoured you. And, after all, you could not write to Lord Ashbury yourself. You are an unmarried woman."

Ruth turned her fulminating gaze on Drew. "As it is, you have dragged him all the way for no reason. Between the Prince Regent and the Duchess of Haverford, Lady Ashbury and the Weasel have lost their audience."

"Nonetheless," Val insisted, no less firm for being quiet, "I needed to know. I have no idea who this Weasel is and how he plays into the trouble, but Elspeth Ashbury is my responsibility, the widow of my brother, using my position, my house, and my financial support to destroy my reputation and the reputation of an innocent lady."

His words punctured Ruth's ire. Had she been so protective of her own feelings that she'd forgotten his? "I am sorry, Val. Lord Ashbury. I did not consider… I should have written to you."

His smile was uncertain, though his tone was warm. "I am here now, Lady Ruth. Shall we share what has been done, and what is yet to do?" He raised an eyebrow. "I take it that all present are part of this strategy session? What of Lady Zyba? And *Sederke* Jeyhun?"

See how wonderful he is? Ruth wanted to say. *How unlike those look down their noses at those who have cast their lives in with ours? Those who treat them as servants?*

When Val asked about the retainers, the duke rewarded him with a satisfied nod and then glanced at the quiet brother, introduced as Barnabas. At a flick of his father's finger, Lord Barnabas left the room by a door in one of the side walls of the room.

Val could easily believe that the duke had been a king and a general. He exuded power; a sense of absolute confidence in his own abilities and in the fealty of those around him. Wellington had a similar aura. Men of all ranks followed him willingly into hell, and women adored him.

Lord Barnabas returned, followed by the two Easterners Val knew and one more, an older man.

The duke performed the introductions. "My advisor and friend, Yousef ibn Ahmed. Yousef Bey, Lord Ashbury." The man called Yousef shook hands in the Western style, his grip firm. Was Bey a title? Part of his name? Val would ask Jeyhun or Drew when he had a chance.

The duke went on, "Zyba and Jeyhun, you have already met. They speak highly of you, Ashbury."

Val bowed.

The duke invited everyone to sit, and set out his plan for the meeting. "I propose that I explain what we have been doing, Ashbury, and that you then tell us the measures you are taking. Is that acceptable?"

It was polite of him to ask, but Val wondered how often he encountered people who would correct or deny his plans. Val was certainly not going to do so. "Please proceed, Your Grace."

The Winshires seemed to have everything in hand. The Prince Regent himself had made it clear he placed no credence in the rumours, and no less a personage than the Duchess of Haverford had scolded Elspeth and told her to stop. Lady Sutton, the wife of the duke's heir, had marshalled a formidable company of Society's matrons to counter the rumours with quiet scorn, and to show their belief in Ruth's innocence by inviting her to their events. And the duke and his sons had managed to corner their cousin at one of those events and, as Winshire put it, "discuss the matter like gentlemen."

A snort of laughter from Drew, quickly repressed, hinted at the nature of the discussion.

"It is almost a pity you cut Weasel off without a penny after he tried to kill you, Kaka," Lord Sutton mused. "With no possibility of threatening his income, a threat to his manhood seemed the most likely to succeed."

The duke ignored the chuckles from others in the room and spoke to Val. "I take it you came to Brighton with a plan?"

"Yes, Your Grace." Though one part of it was already in ashes. He ought to be delighted that Ruth had cleared her name without need for any drastic measures, but he had hoped the situation might make her family amenable to a union with a poor specimen like him.

"I saw my solicitor while I was in London. By now, if my reading of the man is correct, he will have written to my sister-in-law to tell her that she no longer has the use of my London townhouse nor access to my accounts. I cannot, and do not wish to, touch her allowance as my brother's widow, and I will provide her with accommodation in lieu of the dower house at Ashbury Hall, but all else ends."

The duke's eyes narrowed. "You think the solicitor is her man?"

"I am certain of it. I've left him on notice that I'll be returning to London to review every action he has taken on my behalf since I became earl, and warning him to have the books ready. I fully expect him to have absconded by the time I return." He grinned. Several former soldiers were pleased to take his coin in return for the favour of finding out where the solicitor went to and making sure that anything of Val's he took was retrievable.

"You'll just let him go?" Sutton asked.

Jeyhun laughed. "He is having him watched, Jamie Bey. You are, Val, are you not?"

Val tipped his head in acknowledgement, and the duke gave one short decisive nod. "Well done, Ashbury."

Val shrugged. "My neglect. My problem. I will visit my sister-in-law this afternoon. I take it you can give me her direction? The solicitor was not forthcoming."

Ruth still looked strained, as if the conversation hadn't pleased her, or as if she was waiting for something unpleasant. No one had mentioned the usual remedy for a scandal involving an unmarried man and a single woman. Should Val? No. She was so independent that she might withdraw from Society altogether rather than submit to a forced marriage.

And, though he was sure their friendship could survive such a rocky start, he didn't want to force her. He wanted her to choose him freely, never mind that she was more likely to use that freedom to reject him.

He wouldn't give up on the dream that had driven him to Brighton as much as the concern that Ruth was in trouble. He listened and even participated in the rest of what had indeed become a strategy session. He accepted Drew's company on the visit to Elspeth—a visible statement that the Winshires and Ashbury were aligned. He agreed to all the Winshire family's ideas for rehabilitating him in Brighton Society and later in London, including the duke's offer to arrange an invitation to the Marine Pavilion to be presented to the Prince Regent.

With all the suggested entertainments and activities for both him and the girls, he'd be spending plenty of time with Ruth. His challenge would be to court her under the watchful eyes of her family. Perhaps, after all, he should start by seeking a private meeting with the duke.

22

———

How dare Ashbury do this to her! To think that Elspeth had argued against Stanley's plan, though she'd had to agree to it in the end. Denying Stanley was not safe.

However, since receiving the solicitor's letter this morning, she could hardly wait to put it into practice. Throwing her out into the street? Slashing her income to a pittance? How dare he! After all the sacrifices she had made for the earldom—shut away in the country for months at a time and claiming Isabelle's squalling brat, all so that Ashbury might have his heir—she deserved pleasant company and pretty things around her.

She would have had them, too, and for a lifetime, if her husband had not been a fool with his horses and had lived just a few months longer; if the younger Ashbury had had the decency to die; if Isabelle had just kept her head when the man turned up so unexpectedly. The local wisewoman had assured her Isabelle was carrying a son, not another useless daughter. Elspeth would have been mother to the earl, her position unassailable, and she would have found a way to make sure that Ashbury expired of his wounds.

Ashbury would pay. The Winderfield woman, too. Stanley had been furious to learn that the Duchess of Haverford had come to the bitch's rescue. Ruth Winderfield would have to pay. They would all have to pay. Windy was even now out on her errand, setting the plot into motion.

Chloe Harwood had let her down, too. As recently as two weeks ago, the stupid woman had reported that Ashbury was still a recluse, but she must have lied, for he had been to London, was here in Brighton! And with no warning from Chloe. Such treachery was not to be tolerated, but Chloe would keep. First, Ashbury needed to be destroyed. Then, Elspeth would decide what to do about Chloe. A few rumours about her and a handsome footman? No. A groom. Given Harwood was fonder of his horses than his wife, a groom would be a much better choice!

Imagining her revenge cheered Elspeth briefly, but the mood was interrupted by the knocker, and then the butler's voice at the door. She had left instructions that she was not at home to visitors, but she had assumed that Ashbury would bully his way inside, and he did.

She was ready for him. Ready to apologise prettily for believing the Harwood woman's lies. Ready to promise to do everything she could to support him in Society. Ready to beg for the company of her dear little daughter. Stanley had another plan if Elspeth couldn't get her hands on the chit, but there was a certain poetic justice in using Isabelle's bastard to bend Isabelle's widower to her will.

23
___

"I don't trust her any more than I'd trust an adder," Val told Ruth, when he and Drew escorted her and Lady Rosemary to the theatre later that evening. "If I refuse to let her see Genny and Mirrie, though, she'll turn it against us. What reason can I give? That she is a bad mother? That she isn't Genny's mother at all? That she might be aunt to both the girls, but that she abandoned them three years ago and has shown no interest in them since? All true, but they could be turned to hurt Genny. Mirrie, too."

Ruth could see his point. "A supervised visit?"

Val nodded. "Tomorrow afternoon, on the Steyne. I'll be there. Crick and Nanny Pansy, too. I wondered if you…?"

"Of course," Ruth agreed.

The carriage pulled up at the theatre, and Ruth could see Val brace himself for the crowds. He managed well, though, and even recognised a comrade from his former regiment, a Colonel Rutledge, who greeted him with delight, though he coughed and looked wooden when Val presented him to Ruth and her brother and sister.

Drew took the opportunity to say, in a loud voice, "It was good of Val to come down to help us scotch these foolish rumours about him and my sister. All because we called in on him on our way through the Midlands!"

Rutledge took the conversation ball and lobbed it back. "I've been telling my wife that Val is as sane as any of us, and as good a man as you could ever wish to have at your right hand in a tight place."

"You're married, Rutledge?"

"Yes, just a few months ago. And I had better finish finding Lady Rutledge the refreshments I promised and get back to her. May I bring her by your box to meet one of the best officers I ever had?"

He was as good as his word, and turned up in the next interval with his wife on his arm. Sophia whispered that she was one of the Redepenning family, a relative of the Earl of Chirbury and the only female in a family of army and navy officers. She was, herself, the widow of a sailor. Ruth hadn't met her, but then, the Redepennings were family connections of the Haverfords, and the Duke of Haverford had decreed that his family and her father's must not mix.

The prohibition did not appear to concern Lord and Lady Rutledge. They lingered in the Winshire box, and others who knew them soon followed. Val and Rutledge compared notes as younger brothers landed with a title after the death of an elder. "No condolences necessary," Rutledge said bluntly. "The man was a monster."

Lady Rutledge had heard all the rumours about Ruth and Val, and bluntly asked for more details. "Elspeth Ashbury is a liar, of course, and Weasel Winderfield has never forgiven the Duke of Winshire for having the audacity to live, but when one goes to bat for a man greatly admired by one's husband, being armed with the facts would be useful. Lord Ashbury does not seem insane to me. Nor do I think that you, Lady Ruth, would be easily taken in by a rogue."

Drew laughed. "Anyone would have to be quite insane to attempt to compromise either of my sisters, especially with me, her companion, and half a dozen of our horsemen at hand to see to her honour."

Lady Rutledge's smile put Ruth in mind of a cat who has just commandeered a cream pot. "That little morsel of information clearly slipped the attention of those spreading the worst of the rumours. Thank you, Lord Andrew. I know just the tone of scorn to use when dropping that fact in the next 'tear your neighbours to shreds in the name of morality' session."

"You have useful allies, Ashbury," Drew commented on the way home. "Rutledge is highly regarded, and Lady Rutledge has connections at the highest levels of both army and navy as well as throughout the aristocracy."

Val smiled, but it was a distracted curve of the lips. He must be tired, of course, being out late tonight after days of travel. And Ruth supposed he was worried about tomorrow. Presumably, it was something to do with managing Lady Ashbury that made him ask to speak privately with Ruth's father when they arrived back at the house. Ruth was a little piqued not to be included, but Val declined Drew's company, too. So perhaps it was some other matter entirely that he wished to discuss.

Ruth assured herself that Val would tell her what he wanted her to know. It was not as if she owned him, after all. And on the fit of disgruntlement that thought caused, she went up to bed rather than carrying out her original plan of waiting in the hall until he was finished, to wish him a good night.

24

———

Elspeth hadn't expected an opportunity at the plan's very first step, and there hadn't been one. Ashbury had hovered through the whole meeting, and the brat Genevieve was shy and awkward. Ashbury brought the Winderfield woman with him, too, and Isabelle's other chit, Mirabelle. Isabelle had insisted on that name, a mix of her own and Ashbury's mother's. Ashbury—Elspeth's Ashbury—had supported her. The little demon glowered at Elspeth through the whole meeting which, given she was the picture of Isabelle at the same age, made Elspeth's skin crawl.

Still, she stayed long enough to flatter and cajole Genevieve into a smile, and to introduce the brat to Windy. She hoped she had done enough to make the silly little thing susceptible to the second step in the plan.

25

______

Val couldn't help but think it was the calm before the storm. He could not complain about his acceptance by the Brighton social scene, Elspeth's seeming conversion to an amiable penitent, anxious to show her true remorse for past failings, or the warmth of his inclusion in the Winshire contingent.

But the first annoyed him because he knew how fickle Society could be, Elspeth was a liar to her bones and he didn't trust such a wholesale reformation, and acceptance by Winshire and family, while something to be treasured for itself, wasn't getting him any closer to Ruth. Indeed, as his first week in Brighton drifted into a second, he saw less and less of the warm friend he so treasured and more and more of the mask she donned for company.

To be fair, they were in company more often than not, thanks to the need to restore her reputation and his own. Sophia—he was now on first-name terms with all of Ruth's brothers and sisters— decreed that he should not single Ruth out in any way, lest people remember their supposed inappropriate association.

Val bowed to Sophia's social expertise, but how was he to convince Ruth to overlook all his flaws and marry him if he couldn't even court her?

"Your turn, Ashbury."

Val shook off his introspection to focus on the billiard table. Rutledge had gathered several old acquaintances from their military days for an afternoon around the baize, and Val should have been enjoying it; would have been enjoying it except for the heavy feeling deep in his gut that spoke of disaster to come.

He managed to make a creditable job of sinking a few balls, and even to laugh at a few jokes and jeer at some tall stories. The weight in his gut grew over the next hour. In the billiards room with the drapes drawn and the hum of conversation, he hadn't been aware of the rain, and a loud crack of thunder had more than one of these battle-hardened warriors catching themselves as they began to crouch. The sound was almost a relief to Val. Perhaps the weather was all that was wrong with him. Hard on that thought came another. "Crick."

"What's 'Crick'?" asked one of the other guests.

"His old servant, I think he means," Rutledge said. "He's still with you, then?"

Val nodded. "I'll have to ask you to excuse me, Rutledge. Thunderstorms… bother him."

From the thoughtful nods, most of the men in the room knew what he meant.

"It's time I left, too. My wife will have my head if I'm not home in time to escort her to her parents for dinner."

One by one, the others gave their own reasons for leaving, but when they passed the windows to the drawing room on their way to the entrance hall, it was clear that the rain was heavier than expected. Lady Rutledge had seen the problem before any of them, for the butler was there to point them to half a dozen large umbrellas. "Her ladyship suggests one between two, my lords, gentlemen," he said, handing them out as the guests sorted themselves into pairs who were heading in a similar direction.

Val hesitated. He had the furthest to go, and—now that the door was open—the thunder rolled on and on. He firmly squelched the part of him that wanted to gibber under the nearest bed. As he took a pace towards the servant with the umbrellas, the men in the doorway were pushed unceremoniously out of the way by one of

Winshire's warriors, wild-eyed, heaving for breath, and calling his name.

The man held Mirrie on his hip, clinging to his shoulders, but as soon as she saw Val, she reached out for him. "Papa! Help Genny!"

In less than a blink, she was in his arms, burrowing her head into his chest, clinging to him as if she feared being torn away. "I have you, Mirrie. I have you," he murmured, patting her back, all the while looking his questions at Winshire's retainer.

The man had slumped as Mirrie leapt from him to Val, but he drew himself up. "An attack, my lord, as the little ladies were heading home after their walk. We saw, and went after them, but there were too many. They got away with Lady Genny. Lady Ruth is following them with one of my comrades. She sent me to find you."

The account left a hundred questions, but they could wait. "Which way did they go?" Val asked.

The warrior shook his head. "Up the beach, my lord, and then inland. After that?" He shrugged. "But our princess will send word to the house of my khan. I must go and be ready."

"Wait. I am coming with you. Rutledge, can you loan me a horse?"

Rutledge nodded. "My wife has already gone to give the order. And I'm coming too."

A chorus of agreement came from the other old campaigners. Winshire's man glanced around and the corner of his mouth turned up. "You have your own army, Lord Ashbury. Between yours and ours, the one the Weasel has gathered will be outclassed, I think."

"What has Weasel Winderfield to do with this?" Val asked.

"It was he who took Lady Genny. There was thunder. Your man Crick—he…" The warrior stopped, searching for words.

"He dropped under the nearest cover and lost all sense of where he was," Val guessed.

A nod. "Your woman, the nursemaid? She bent over him. At that moment, the Weasel ran up to the girls. He and one of the men with them caught the girls up, but by then we were upon them. My lady managed to down the one who held Lady Mirrie, and we dealt with three more, but by then the Weasel and the rest of them were gone."

"You will rescue her, Papa?" Mirrie begged.

"Of course, my love," Val soothed, hoping it was true. "Rutledge, may I impose on you to go to my sister-in-law's house and hold her there for the magistrate? If Weasel is involved, so is she."

Lady Rutledge spoke up, her quiet voice nonetheless catching the attention of all in the hall. "I will go with you, Gil. And perhaps two others?" She looked around the group. "I have ordered all our riding horses to be saddled and brought to the front. I've also asked the next-door neighbour for the loan of his horses, so that should make seven in all. We will take the cabriolet, since Lady Ashbury's house is on the other side of town, and I take it time is of the essence."

Soon, they were on their way, Mirrie—soaked through and shivering—still clinging to Val. He couldn't take her into battle, but he didn't want to let her go while she was so distressed.

Fifteen minutes later, they entered the mews of the Winshire townhouse, where the duke waited, already mounted, amid a sea of horses and warriors, both men and women. Rosemary came out of the crowd and solved at least one of his problems, holding up her arms for Mirrie.

"Come to me, darling, and let your father get ready to go and save Genny. There may be fighting, and he needs to know you are safe so he can concentrate on the rescue. I've sent for your Nanny Pansy, who will be worrying about you, and you shall stay with me until we have Genny safely home."

Thankfully, Mirrie didn't argue. She turned her face up for a kiss, then dropped down into Rosemary's arms.

And just in time, for at that moment, another of the Winshire retainers, this one dishevelled and blown, stumbled into the courtyard, blood welling between the fingers that clutched one shoulder. He fell to his knees before the duke's horse, shouting something in a foreign tongue.

Jamie, Ruth's older brother, knelt to lift him to his feet, asking rapid questions in the same language, and around them the rest of the Winshire contingent burst into activity, some mounting their horses, some moving between Val and his friends handing out a veritable armoury of weapons. "Better conceal these," Val suggested. "We don't want to make the Prince Regent nervous."

"Why don't I let him know what is going on?" Major Jacobs was an equerry in Prinny's household. "What is going on?" he added.

The duke heard. "We've just learned that Lady Ashbury is the sister of a notorious criminal. We suspect he has used Weasel and his sister to enact a revenge against the Winshires for a defeat last year. Tell your master that the Duke of Winshire and the Earl of Ashbury are leading a rescue for Lady Genevieve Monforte and Lady Ruth Winderfield, who have been kidnapped by the Duke of Devil's Kitchen."

"Lady Ruth?" Val hadn't thought his heart could clench tighter, but he'd been wrong.

"Yes. She and Kenjai here were ambushed, and she was taken. But we know the road they were on, and we think we know where they were heading."

26

A child was whimpering. Ruth struggled to focus her mind, or even just to open her eyes. Something—perhaps the pounding headache or the roiling nausea—blocked her awareness of her surroundings. Only the cries of the child broke through her confusion.

Ruth used the sound as a rope to drag herself to full consciousness, ignoring the complaints of her body, which multiplied as she became more and more aware.

She cautiously lifted one lid. Being thought unconscious might give her a chance to work out what was going on. The room was small and shabby, and poorly lit, but as far as she could see, the only other person present was curled into a tiny ball on a bed against the opposite wall, crying in shuddering sobs, as if she had spent hours grieving and no longer had any hope of comfort.

Ruth could hear no one else. She opened the other eye and warily shifted her head. She and the child were alone in the room. She shifted to sit up and go to the child, but her legs and arms resisted, heavy fetters pulling at her ankles and wrists.

By now, she'd remembered enough to know who shared her room. She and the one guardsman left to her had been clinging onto the back of the carriage abducting Genny Monforte when outriders had seen them. There'd been too many assailants to fight off. Kenjai had been able to fight free, and she had yelled at him to go just as she was felled by a blow to the head. It had taken a second blow to knock her unconscious, and before that, she'd heard a shot. Had Kenjai got away? She could hope.

"Genny?" she said, keeping her voice low. She couldn't do anything about peepholes and lurking listeners, but she didn't have to make it easy for them.

The little girl's face emerged from her arms, her eyes red and swollen. "Lady Ruth? I thought you were dead!"

"Oh, darling." Ruth held out her arms and Genny burst into tears again, lifting an ankle to show that she, too, was shackled to the bed. The fetter was a leather strap. Perhaps, if they weren't watching, she could get free. She tugged both arms into her line of sight. Leather, yes but chained firmly so that she could not bring them together, or even reach her wrist with her mouth.

"Your uncle and my father will come for us," she assured Genny. Not that she was counting on a rescue. The families would search, of course. Two of her escort and Mirrie had got away, and Val's servants, too, knew they'd been taken. But she couldn't count on them finding her and Genny before whoever was responsible killed them, hurt them, or moved them elsewhere.

Her eyes roamed the room. There was little to catalogue. Two iron bedsteads with thin mattresses and no blankets. Between them, a small barred window letting in a dismal light, with a table under it on which stood a candle, unlit, and a bowl and tumbler. Opposite the window, the room's door.

Her gaze returned to the tumbler, and the most insistent of her pains instantly became her dry mouth and throat. She tried to reach the tumbler, but it was on Genny's side of the table, and the chain attached to the leather strap at her wrist did not give her enough play. It seemed looser than the other, but a few minutes struggle made it clear that her hand was not going to pass through the loop.

"Genny, dearest, is there water in the tumbler? Can you reach it and pass it to me? Be very, very quiet. We don't want the bad people to hear us."

The child scrambled up onto her knees and crawled up the bed.

They had only secured her by the one leg, and had given her a longer chain. She reached the tumbler, but she couldn't get it to Ruth's mouth. She even climbed down off the bed, balancing the tumbler with extreme care, but it was no use. The closest she could come was still inches away, hand outstretched, and with Ruth bent towards her as far as her chains would allow.

"The spoon!" Genny said. "I can put some water on the spoon!" She put the tumbler carefully by the leg of the bed and clambered back up so she could reach the bowl on the table. She wrinkled her lips in disgust. "I will wipe it. It is covered in fat. The soup was *disgusting.*"

"There is fat?" Ruth asked.

"Horrid fat. And the soup is cold, now, so it is all thick and gluggy."

"Genny, I have an idea. Can you get a spoonful of that fat and rub it on my hand and my wrist? If we can make them slippery, I might be able to pull my hand out."

It took several trips back for more fat, but in the end, Ruth could feel the leather sliding as she pulled at her hand. She tucked her thumb as far into the palm as she could, thumb and fingers all straight, her hand curled, and then tugged on her arm. The leather slid up, then stuck on the bone at the base of her thumb. She tugged harder, harder still, and suddenly her hand came away, aching and scraped, but free.

Genny squeaked in delight, then slapped both hands over her mouth and turned scared eyes on the door.

After a moment, Ruth turned and began to work on the buckle at the other wrist, but a padlock prevented her access. A knife, perhaps? She could cut the leather loops that secured the padlock onto the buckle.

Her knife was not in its sheaf on her thigh. She felt in the knot of hair at the back of her head. Aha! They had missed her spare. It wasn't much. Not even six inches long, and no bigger across than her little finger, but pulled from the wooden sheath that disguised it as an ornamental pin, it was as sharp as a sword.

She sawed away at the leather. It seemed to take hours, but must have been only minutes, before the last loop gave. She worked the leather tongue into the buckle until it gave enough for her to free the shank from the whole and undo the fetter.

Genny was sitting on the other bed by now, watching, and bouncing silently in delight. "The tumbler," Ruth asked, and the girl slid down to oblige. They clasped hands for a moment, while Ruth savoured the few mouthfuls of water left in the container.

The buckles on the ankles were harder still, even with the use of both hands. But at last Ruth was free, and able to release Genny, and pause for a long hug, which she needed nearly as much as the child.

Now to get out of the room. They'd been left undisturbed so far, which probably meant no hidden watchers, but that didn't mean no one would come to check on them.

At this point, a true hairpin was what she needed, and she had several. Setting the knife beside her on the floor, she set to work on the door lock. It was cheap and old, and gave up its secrets in moments. Ruth said a prayer of thanks for Drew, who had learned the trick of it in some disreputable way he would never explain, and taught it to her.

With Genny tucked safely behind her, Ruth peeked out into the hall. The first thing to meet her eye was a bulky shoulder, but the rattling snore reassured her. She emerged a little more. A passage-way, with doors each side. Beside this one, a large man sprawled asleep in a chair. Beyond him, she could see the head of a flight of stairs going down.

"Wait here," she whispered to Genny. "I am going to see if that is a way out."

The child trembled, but nodded, and Ruth bent to give her a swift kiss before stepping carefully over the man's legs to creep the rest of the distance to the stairwell. She stopped in the shadow of a doorway, close enough to see another sentinel on the landing, this one wide awake, but luckily focused on something further down the stairs.

She withdrew to Genny. "This way," she whispered. Hand in hand, they hurried quietly in the direction away from the stairs.

The troop that rode out as the sun was setting numbered more than thirty men, all armed. Rutledge and his companions joined them as they left Brighton behind. When they slowed to a walk to rest the horses, his report was succinct. "The bird has flown. She was collected in a carriage in the early afternoon. She told her household to pack up and meet her in London. Where are we going?"

Drew, who was riding on Val's other side, answered the question. "A hunting lodge recently made over to the Duke of Devil's Kitchen in payment of a debt. My father gets regular reports on his movements, and we were told he is visiting his new possession."

"You think he has your missing niece? But why?"

Val asked the question that answered Rutledge. "Is it true that the villain is really Elspeth's brother, Wharton?"

Drew nodded. "Yes. My father just had confirmation of that today. He was going to tell you, Val, next time he saw you."

"Stanley Wharton?" Rutledge commented. "That nasty little toad? He was a junior at Eton when I was a senior, and a wart on the face of the earth then. I thought he fled overseas after getting caught up in all sorts of nasty activities. Including flesh trading and treason, so I heard."

The duke must have given a signal, for the riders around them nudged their horses into a trot, and conversation lapsed. Even with two riders at the head of the troop with lanterns to search out the way, a trot was the fastest they could go in the dark and the rain.

Val ignored how wet he was getting, and concentrated on the ride. That, and his constant prayer that they would arrive in time.

In the gloom at the other end of the passageway, Ruth found what she was looking for—a handle notched into the edge of the panel. Opened, it let onto a servant stair, as she had hoped.

Down they went, into the darkness, Ruth feeling for each step, and Genny holding onto her skirt and following close behind. When Ruth's searching foot found a flat surface that showed the stair had ended, she hunted the wall for another catch, but before she released it, she heard voices.

The first voice was Lady Ashbury's. "We should have left the Winderfield bitch on the road, Stanley. We don't need a war with the Duke of Winshire."

"Winshire started the war," a man's voice answered. "I am merely upping the stakes. Once we get his precious daughter into my territory, we'll see who is giving orders to whom. If he is very good, I might return the chit intact." He giggled. "Or mostly intact."

"I didn't want any part of this." Ruth recognised the whine as Weasel. "I was only trying to help Elspeth get her daughter back. You told me you missed her, Elspeth, but you don't even want her, do you?"

Ruth felt Genny stiffen beside her, and had only just thought about covering the poor little girl's ears when Elspeth replied, "I want the money Ashbury will give me for her. Think of the fun we shall have, Windy. In America, perhaps. The colonies might be quite tolerable with a large wad of cash."

"Go to bed the pair of you, and stop bickering," the man called Stanley commanded. "We will leave tomorrow at first light. I want to be back in London before those fools in Brighton can search this far." He giggled again. "Don't forget to kiss your precious little daughter good night, sister dear."

If Lady Ashbury checked, she would find them gone, but would she? Ruth hoped they could count on her continuing disinterest. Even so, she led Genny up the stairs as swiftly as she could while staying quiet. Up and up they went in the darkness, until the stairs ran out at a door. It let into a narrow corridor. Ruth stood and listened, but she couldn't hear a sound. Surely if people were up here, there'd be some light? Some noise?

She led the way down the corridor, checking behind each door, her tension easing as each disclosed only a tiny servant's room or a slightly larger dormitory, empty in the light that trickled in through the dormer windows as a half-moon drifted fitfully in and out of the clouds. Light enough, that was, to her dark-accustomed eyes.

She'd found the attics, which were empty as she had hoped. Whatever this house was, it was largely unused. Reassured they were alone, Ruth checked each room more thoroughly, and examined the windows for one that would open onto a part of the roof they could escape to at need.

Finally, she decided on a tiny room at the very end of the corridor. She stacked a few bottles she had found in front of the door from the staircase, where they would be knocked over with a crash if the door was opened, then added more partway along the corridor. Finally, she closed herself and Genny into the room she'd chosen.

"Let's try to get some sleep," she suggested. Unlikely, what with thirst, pain, and worry. But at least she could rest and Genny might sleep. Still, their luck was holding. Clearly, Lady Ashbury had not attempted to see Genny, or the alarm would already have been sounded. Please God, let rescue arrive before they were missed, for their hiding place would not stand up to a proper search.

27

———

The rain eased in the early hours of the morning. The road to the hunting lodge had proved hard to find in the dark, but they knew how far away it should be from Brighton and went back and back over half an hour of road, following every hint of a track.

Then the moon slipped from the clouds as they were covering the same ground they'd been over twice, and a sharp-eyed rider called out to the duke, "Your Grace. Someone has swept the ground here!"

With lamp and moonlight on the ground, the story was easy to read. A carriage and horses had turned in here, apparently passing through a solid block of shrubbery. In moments, willing hands had cleared the way—what appeared to be a barrier was cut branches, piled eight feet high and fifteen wide, already wilting.

The duke sent scouts ahead on foot, slipping through the forest on either side of the carriageway the clearance had disclosed. Now came the worst part of any battle: waiting to engage the enemy, short on information and long on discomfort. The dismounted warriors, British and Pari-Daisan, saw to their horses, conversed in whispers, refreshed themselves from flasks, checked their weapons.

The pistols they had given Val had remained dry in the saddlebag under his knee, and everything needed to reload them was wrapped in oiled cloth inside a leather pouch—no problems there.

The minutes dragged. Val had to keep reining in his imagination, which fed him images of Ruth violated and murdered, Genny hurt and alone. His fears could not be allowed to overwhelm him. Instead, he channelled them to fuel his anger—not a hot rage that would impair his judgement, but a cold stern wrath at any who dared threaten those he loved.

At last, one of the scouts returned, and the leaders of the expedition—the duke, Jamie Winderfield, Rutledge and Val, gathered to hear their report. The crime lord, it appeared, travelled with a veritable army. The scouts had taken out six sentries, and barricaded an unknown number of other men into the stables. The house was substantial: several stories with attics above. It was impossible to know whether the one sentry who was talking was telling the truth when he claimed more than two dozen men were inside with their master. If so, the rescuers would have to be very sure they could reach the hostages before the villains did.

At the duke's suggestion, they rode the rest of the way to the house to question the captured sentries themselves, and to see the lay of the land.

Every strategy had risks, as the duke said when he summed up the discussion that followed. "We don't have any idea where in the house our ladies are being kept. If we break in, they may be hurt before we can get to them. If we wait until morning, or whenever Wharton chooses to emerge, our ladies may be suffering right now, and we'll be standing by while it happens."

Val had been examining the house from where they stood in the cover of the stables. "What if we could get in from the top? Find an empty room in the attics and enter that way? If we could get even a couple of people inside, and they could find our ladies…?"

"It would be a tough climb," Rutledge mused, his eyes narrowing as he considered the idea.

"I could do it," Drew offered. "It's our best chance, Kaka. If we can find our ladies and take out their guard, we can defend them while the rest of you make a full-on assault."

The duke gave a sharp nod, and Drew fell into a quiet conversation with one of his warriors, while the pair of them removed their gloves, their jackets, their boots and their stockings. "Kaka, we'll ascend between the porch pillars and the side of the house, then walk that bit of pediment, climb up where that wing meets the main house, and make our way to the roof. We should be able to drop down to that bit of roof by the gable there." He pointed to each feature as he named it. "The window is slightly open, so there may be someone inside. We'll make a decision on whether to enter or keep looking once we've got up there. Once we're inside, watch for us to signal that we've found the ladies."

The duke nodded again. "And then we'll attack. We will be ready, my son."

Val watched in agonised envy as Drew and his companion ascended the house face, taking it in turns to lead, the lower one often offering a foothold for the other, who then would pause to reach back for his partner. *I should be doing that.* But even when he had both hands, he couldn't climb the way those two did.

"They are quite mad," Jamie murmured in his ear. "Back at home, they used to climb rockfaces for fun. Still do. The pair of them are making a list of all the mountains in Wales and Scotland with climbs they consider worth doing."

Around them, the men dispersed, one group to each face of the house, to choose windows to break through when the signal came. Val stayed, watching the climbers approach the attic window.

They were almost there when the window opened wide, and someone leaned out of it. Val stepped out of the shadow, staring. "Ruth!" It was. She and Drew were embracing through the open window, and then she stepped back out of sight and returned to help Genny climb out of the window into Drew's waiting arms.

He settled the child on his back, clinging like a monkey, and Ruth followed her out the window. "What is she doing?" Jamie asked. "Ah! I see." Ruth had taken off her pelisse and her shoes and stockings. She looped her skirt up between her legs and bound it in place by tying her pelisse around her waist by the sleeves. She used her sash to tie Genny to Drew's back.

Val waited, his heart in his mouth. Drew led the way down, Ruth following, and his friend bringing up the rear, helping Ruth whenever she had trouble making progress. Never had five minutes moved so slowly, but at last Drew set one foot and then another onto the ground, and Val was there to untie his little girl and take her in his arms.

Winshire helped Ruth down the last several feet, and enfolded her in his embrace, then passed her to her eldest brother. Val would have liked to hug her, too, but had to be satisfied with words. "My lady, I cannot find the words to tell you how glad I am to see you."

She was grinning broadly. "The feeling is entirely mutual, Lord Ashbury." She untied her pelisse and untucked her skirts, letting them fall to hide her legs.

"What can you tell us about the situation in the house?" Winshire asked. "Now that you're safe, we can make our assault."

Val hugged Genny to him while he listened, revelling in her presence, her arms tightly wound around his neck. In the past few hours, he'd sensed the void her loss would leave in his life. He wasn't sure he could face another such bereavement. As for the loss of Ruth! Coming so close to a grief beyond any he'd known had brought him clarity. Worthy or not, he needed her, his longing a constant pain. The choice must be hers, of course, but he couldn't live with himself if he didn't tell her how he felt.

Focus, Val. Battle first. Talk to Ruth afterwards.

After the anxious hours, the attack itself was an anti-climax. Most of the crime lord's men, faced with a determined and disciplined force of well-armed trained soldiers, surrendered or fled. The few who fought were not hard to overwhelm.

Ruth was mostly an onlooker, kept from the battle by the need to protect Genny. Once the child was reassured she was safe, she had fallen asleep again, her head on Ruth's lap where she sat on the ground, leaning her back against an outbuilding, a sword in one hand and a loaded pistol close beside.

Ruth almost fell asleep herself, as she waited, startled back to full consciousness occasionally as an escaping miscreant was apprehended close by, or when one of her brothers took time from the fight to let her know what was happening.

"We've secured the ground floor."

"Lady Elspeth and Weasel are in custody. We haven't found Wharton yet."

"We have Wharton boxed in, and are clearing the rooms either side of where he and the last of his men are holding out."

On that third occasion, Drew brought her two boys of perhaps eleven or twelve, richly dressed in silks but barefooted and with vacant expressions and the weary eyes of sad old men. Each was still wearing an ankle shackle. "We found these two chained to beds in one of the rooms near Wharton. Look after them, will you? Boys, sit here."

The two of them sat immediately, dropping like puppets whose strings had been released, and transferred their intent gaze from Drew to Ruth, watching her every move. She shifted Genny's head onto a folded blanket one of her brothers had brought her earlier, and pulled her knife from her hair. "Let's see if we can get those ankle straps off, shall we?"

They flinched at the sight of the knife, but Ruth kept talking as she held first one ankle and then the other, and carefully cut away the leather that held the padlock so she could open the buckle. She tucked them under another of the blankets. The morning wasn't particularly cool, but nor was it warm enough for those silk shirts and pantaloons.

They sat passively under her ministrations, cuddling together. "What are your names?" she asked, but they stared at her, mutely, then hid their faces in the blankets when a din rose from the house —shouts, screams, gunfire.

In the chaos, four men climbed out of a nearby window and saw her and the children. "Hostages," one of them shouted, and they turned in her direction. She took one down with the pistol, but the other three came on, spreading out, laughing when she brandished the sword.

Their jeering turned to obscene curses when she pinked the nearest in his shoulder, only missing his throat because he swerved at the last second. Sobered, taking her more seriously, two of them attempted to crowd her away from the children, the other to creep around behind her.

She managed to hold her ground and fend off the first two attacks, but then they struck at once and the loaned sword shattered. The three villains stopped to jeer, and that was their downfall. From the darkness to her left came the shout *Alys-Calys*. Exchange.

Almost without thought, her hand shot up and the hilt of a sword landed in it. Good balance. A little large for her, but she could work with it. Even as she thought, she lunged forward. The villains had turned at the shout, facing Val who was bearing down on them from the gloom.

In moments, it was over, he and she picking up the dance of swords as if they had practiced together a lifetime, like her and Zyba. As others joined them to drag away the bodies, living and dead, Jamie brought her another boy, this one wrapped in Jamie's coat and wearing nothing else. The two already with her shifted to open the blanket to bring him into their cocoon.

"We have Wharton." He wrinkled his nose in disgust. "This one was in the cur's bed." He brushed his hand over his face and yawned. "We've secured the house, Ruth. If you and the children come into the kitchen by the fire, Val has the wounded there for you to look at. We're going to take the stables next."

Ruth gathered Genny into her arms, and the boys followed docilely at her command. She found the kitchen door where Jamie indicated, and led her little procession into a warm cavernous room, where half a dozen men, some English, some Pari-Daisan, sat at the long wooden table. Val took Genny from her arms, and the child stirred and snuggled into his neck. "Come by the fire," he told the boys, leaving Ruth to ask, "Who is bleeding the most?"

Fortunately, no one had sustained more than flesh wounds and bruises. Ruth ripped up tablecloths from a supply in the kitchen's scullery, and bound the wounds. She sent one of the least wounded to find needle and thread, which she boiled before setting stitches in a couple of the worst cuts. But none of it took long.

Before she had finished the first lot, the men trapped in the stable had surrendered and a few more injured men had been sent to the kitchen, some of them prisoners. She carried on, helped by Drew, who was an adequate field medic.

Jamie appeared again to let them know what had been decided. "Lord Rutledge has gone for the local magistrate. Father is sending our people home and the men who came with Val are going to stay as witnesses." Ruth nodded. No need to allow any prejudice against foreigners to confuse who was at fault here.

"I'm sorry, Ruth, but the magistrate will want to talk to you. You, too, Val."

Val was sitting in a chair by the fire, Genny sleeping in his arms, the three boys sitting silently at his feet, alert to every movement in the kitchen. "Can you ask one of your men to take a message to my household to let them know Genny and Ruth are safe?" he asked.

The next stir was the arrival of a troop of militia, sent by the Prince Regent, commanded by a friend of Rutledge's, and instructed to put themselves under the orders of the magistrate.

By this time, Ruth had retrieved the house's cook and a couple of kitchen hands, and set them to work, and everyone had been fed, even the prisoners. Even Wharton had been taken food, though he threw it, plate and all, at the man who delivered it.

By mid-morning, the magistrate had arrived with a small army of hastily sworn in constables. Ruth was the first to give evidence; an unvarnished report of the facts in the style she had been taught when she was a caravan guard. "You managed to release yourself from your bonds," the magistrate asked.

Ruth showed him her bruised and swollen hand. "With the help of the fat from Genny's dinner," she confirmed.

"And picked the lock to get out of the room. An unusual skill for a lady."

Ruth shrugged. "One of my brothers picked the skill up some-where and taught it to the rest of us."

"You then climbed onto the roof to escape and afterwards treated injuries for both your rescuers and the villains who kidnapped you."

Why was he repeating all of this? Did he not believe her? He was shaking his head, but it was in wonder rather than suspicion. "You are a very unusual young woman, Lady Ruth. I am sure it must have been a trial, however. You are free to go. Your father has arranged for you to be escorted back to Brighton with the little girl." He checked his notes. "Lady Genevieve Monforte."

Shaking his head again, he got to his feet and escorted her to the door of the room he was using for the interviews.

The magistrate was systematic and thorough. After interviewing Lady Ruth, he collected testimony from Winshire and those who had ridden with him. Rutledge and his men had handed over to the militia, and were pleased to return to Brighton, but Val asked to remain, and so did Winshire and his two sons.

Val and Winshire were allowed to sit in on the rest of the day's proceedings. "You are here to observe," the magistrate instructed them, not in the least awed by the duke's elevated rank or even his aura of command. "Please leave me to do my job. If you interrupt, I will have you removed."

Next to be interviewed, one by one, were the few servants who had been kept on at the house after it was acquired by Wharton, or hired locally: the stable master and a couple of grooms, the cook, a handful of footmen, three maids. Val was impressed with the way the magistrate used their evidence to decide the order in which to examine the miscreants.

First came those the servants identified as less brutal, less committed to Wharton's interests, or lower in the gang's hierarchy. An offer of lesser charges or even amnesty, provided they cooper-ated, had some of them spilling all the information they had, adding to the picture the magistrate was creating, piece by careful piece.

By now, the magistrate had relaxed enough to discuss each witness with the observers between interviews. As those higher in the gang's hierarchy came before the magistrate, the tone of the interviews changed. Many of them refused to talk at all. Others resorted to obscenity-laden threats. Still, the magistrate garnered a hint there, a fact here, and used them skilfully to elicit further information.

In a break for a meal with just a half a dozen villains left to see,

Winshire commented, "I should tell you that this is not the first time my cousin Wesley Winderfield has worked with the man Wharton." He outlined several attempts at assassination, including an inn fire that could have been fatal for innocent bystanders. "We locked him up after that, until my sons had been confirmed as my heirs, then released him on promise of good behaviour. He has no income, and has—as far as we can tell—been living off the charity of Lady Ashbury, the widow of Lord Ashbury's late brother."

"He should have been prosecuted," the magistrate growled. "You have to take some responsibility for this situation, Your Grace. Taking the law into your own hands like that." A faint smile indicated that the scold amused Winshire, rather than offending him. The magistrate, though, had turned his attention to Val. "Ashbury, what can you tell me about this sister-in-law of yours? Wharton's sister, you said?" All the information Winshire had gleaned about the so-called Duke of Devil's Kitchen had been shared with the magistrate when he arrived. "And the mother of the child that you say was kidnapped. Wasn't her brother just returning the little girl to her?"

Val suddenly saw a path ahead of him to get Elspeth out of Genny's life and begin to undo some of the damage done by the woman's lies, her neglect, and then, in the past twenty-four hours, her abuse of the little girl.

"Elspeth is not Genny's mother," he said. "She and my brother claimed the little girl at birth, but I've recently discovered, from my wife's maid and the midwife who attended the birth, that Genny is my daughter; mine and my wife's."

The magistrate slipped his glasses down his nose and peered at Val over the top of them. "That is rather a large claim, Lord Ashbury."

"It is one of my main reasons for coming to Brighton," Val explained. "To confront my sister-in-law about the theft of my daughter and the intended theft of the baby my wife was carrying when she died." He paused, but the magistrate did not comment.

"My brother had no heir but me, and his wife had been unable to give him a son. I was away with the army. I dread to think what measures they used to force my wife to go along with their scheme…" He shook his head, and the anguish in his voice was very real as he added, "The maid has told me some of it. Poor Isabelle."

"But this is horrific," the magistrate said. "Mind you, it explains why she allowed the poor little girl to be shackled like an animal."

"And why, in the three years since she left Leicestershire, she has never once replied to Genny's monthly letters, and never enquired about her well-being."

The magistrate shook his head. "Horrific. Still, that is not the crime I am here to investigate, Lord Ashbury. You will need to pursue the matter separately. However, I will keep your accusations in mind when I interview the female." He glared over his spectacles. "You will continue to keep your mouth shut, my lord, whatever the temptation to speak, or I shall have you removed." He slipped his spectacles back into place and gave a sharp nod to emphasise the command.

"Yes, sir," Val agreed. "May I ask that, if you consider it helpful, you suggest that her actions show an unsound mind and that, as head of her family, I may need to take that into account in sanctioning her behaviour?"

The magistrate raised an eyebrow, and then grinned. "Yes. Yes, I don't mind that at all. I might just do that. Can't have peers and their wives going around and stealing other people's children."

The following day, back in Brighton, they had to tell Ruth and Rosemary all about it. "Our cousin blamed everyone else," Jamie told them. "He denied any involvement in the kidnapping despite the eyewitnesses, and claimed complete innocence—"

Drew put on a falsetto. "I am only here because Lady Ashbury asked for my company. I had no idea we were meeting a criminal." Then, in his normal voice, he said, "A coward, as well as an idiot."

"Did the magistrate believe him?" Ruth asked. "He struck me as an intelligent man."

"He did not," Val assured her. "Weasel has been sent to the Old Bailey until his trial. Wharton, too, and his London men. Those hired locally will be tried locally."

"And Lady Ashbury?" Ruth asked.

Val allowed himself a grim smile. "Elspeth, too, though—after her performance in front of the magistrate—it's likely we'll be able to get a verdict of unsound mind before the trial, and have her put away where she can do no harm."

Ruth raised her eyebrows. "What happened?

Val shrugged. "I told the magistrate that Genny was my daughter, born to my wife, and that my brother and his wife stole her at her birth, and threatened my wife with dire consequences if she told anyone. It is no more than the truth, as you know. And it is also true that I only discovered the proof of it recently."

Winshire took up the tale, which was just as well, because Val was dwelling on Genny's response when he'd told her this morning, after he arrived home. She had turned to embrace Mirrie, her voice trembling with awe. "We truly are sisters." Val came in for his fair share of hugs, too. "I so much wanted you to be my Papa, and now you are." Tears filled her eyes. "I wish I had known when our Mama was alive. I remember her, Papa. I loved her so much." They had cried together, the three of them, and Nanny Pansy, too, until Val suggested going out for ices on the way to visit Lady Ruth.

Now Val jerked himself back into the present as Winshire explained, "The magistrate played it brilliantly. Lady Ashbury claimed that our Val had been keeping her from Genny, and she was desperate to see the child. He told her he knew she was not the child's mother, had shown no interest in the child since she was born, and had allowed her to be locked away and shackled. He said that he would not be prosecuting her for masquerading as the child's mother, but Val might. She lost her temper. She screamed about the sacrifices she had made, threw around accusations about her sister and her husband—which, I might add, the magistrate is happy to cite as evidence of her hysteria, should Val so desire—and basically admitted everything. Val now has two reputable witnesses, myself and the magistrate, to support his claim that Genny is the child of his marriage."

"As she is," Val pointed out. He had also told the magistrate, and would tell anyone else that might gossip about it, that he had been back in England for a few days at a time in the year that Genny must have been conceived. To London, with no leave and no time to travel except on army business, but no one needed to know his brother had rejected his requests for Isabelle to come and meet him, each time with a different excuse.

They were interrupted by a knock at the door. It was the butler, to announce a messenger from the Marine Pavilion. "For Lady Ruth, Your Grace." Sure enough, a man in the livery of the Prince Regent was ushered in, and bowed before presenting Ruth with a sealed letter on heavy paper. The servant glanced around the room as he waited for Ruth to break the seal, and then crossed to Val. "Lord Ashbury?" Val nodded.

"I am also charged with a letter for you, my lord." He felt inside the satchel he carried and handed it over—to outward appearances, a duplicate of that given to Ruth.

Val opened it and scanned it quickly, interrupted when Ruth said to the servant, "No reply." She curtseyed to her father. "Papa, may I be excused?" Without waiting for an answer, she stalked from the room.

The contents of her letter were the mirror image of his, then. Val sighed and read again more slowly. The Prince Regent meant well, but…

He looked up into the expectant eyes of the lady's family and sighed again. "Please tell His Highness that I thank him for his message," he said to the servant. No point in annoying royalty unnecessarily. He handed the letter to Winshire, and left the room to find Ruth.

A footman sent him upstairs, and another directed him along the hall towards the family wing. He wondered how far he'd be allowed to go before someone turned him back to the public rooms, but then he rounded a corner and heard voices. Ruth's, Genny's, and Mirrie's, with here and there the deeper tones of a boy on the verge of shooting into adulthood. Thomas, the youngest of Winshire's sons.

The first thing he heard was clearly the end of the story of Val's revelations that morning. "And Uncle Val is my true Papa," Genny crowed.

"Genny and I are sisters—That Lady is not Genny's Mama at

all," Mirrie added. "She and I have the same Mama and the same Papa."

"Are you well, Ruth?" asked the boy. "You look upset."

Of course, she was upset, and Val was, too. When she didn't answer Thomas, Val stepped into the room. "Just an impertinent letter," Val told the boy. "Irritating, but not consequential."

Ruth didn't want to giggle. But the way Val characterised a demand from the de-facto monarch of all Britain and its colonies was irresistible balm to her anger. "Not consequential?" She lifted her eyebrows in question. What did he mean? That he had no intention of obeying the Prince's command? It was contrary of her, but that thought wasn't to her taste, either.

"We will make our own decisions," Val said. "Or, rather, you will make your decision and I will support your choice. No one has the right to force your hand. For my own part, I wish I'd already made the opportunity to ask you the question that His Highness has decided you will answer with a 'yes'. I hope you won't refuse me just because you have been instructed to accept."

Her irritation surged back. "First, how petty do you think I am? Second, you haven't asked me anything that I might make a choice about."

Thomas was turning from one speaker to another, like a spectator at tennis. "Oh! Is Val going to ask you to marry him? Oh, good. I like him."

"You marry him, then," Ruth retorted.

She had reckoned without Val's girls, who were hanging one on each hand before she had finished speaking. "Oh please, Lady Ruth," Mirrie begged.

"You would be our mother!" Genny's eyes shone.

"Daughters of mine, let Lady Ruth go, if you please. I have not yet asked Lady Ruth to marry me, and though I am pleased to have your approval, I do not want her badgered. By you or by the Prince Regent."

Thomas's eyes went from Val, to Ruth, to the letter in Ruth's hand, and he opened his mouth again, but Val interrupted. "No more, young Thomas, I beg of you. Your sister is annoyed enough to bury me six feet deep, without you shovelling in more dirt."

Mirrie, who had obeyed her father's command, was now hanging off his arm, whispering loud enough for all to hear, "Go on and ask her, then, Papa." He whispered back, equally loud, "Not while she is cross, sweetheart."

"You should sing her one of your funny songs and tickle her, Papa," Genny advised.

Val snuck a sideways look at Ruth, and she had to laugh at the mixture of mischief and embarrassment in his hopeful smile. "Perhaps I might be allowed to do that one day?" His words were addressed to Genny, but the hint of heat in his eyes was all for Ruth.

"Now," she said.

"My lady?"

"Ask me now, Lord Ashbury."

The heat flared. Then he sank onto one knee and reached inside his coat, withdrawing a small cloth bag. "Lady Ruth Winderfield, since the moment I first met you, I have esteemed you greatly. Every day since, my esteem—let me say, my love—has grown. My life is brighter with you in it, so much so that I dread to face a future without you as my friend, my companion, and my partner. I cannot say that I am worthy to be your husband, but I can say that, if you will be my wife, I will love you every day of my life." He shook the bag over his hand and offered her a dainty ring.

Ruth took it and held it up to examine. "You had the ring ready?" Amethysts formed daisy petals around a central diamond. Finely worked pierced gold in leaves and tendrils formed the mount, and inside the ring, deeply engraved, she read, *My heart is forever thine.*

"I had it made while in London," Val told her. He sounded nervous. Could he doubt her answer? She looked down into his eyes. He remained kneeling at her feet, not turning to look even when the rest of her family came around the corner behind him.

She couldn't stop the smile that spread with the warmth that flooded her. This wasn't a response to the Prince Regent's order that she marry to stop the scandalous rumours about her abduction. He had bought the ring weeks ago. He truly wanted to wed her. He didn't even care that they had an audience. He loved her.

"Do put the poor man out of his misery," Papa suggested.

Ruth sank to her knees, handed Val the ring, and offered him her finger. "Yes. Yes, I will be your wife. I love you."

They had a moment more, as Val slid the ring onto her finger, then they were swamped with congratulations, embraces (from the children), and expressions of relief (from her brothers, who wanted to know what had taken them so long). The laughing, joyful crowd swept them into one of the family sitting rooms, where Winshire sent for champagne.

"You wouldn't let me get her alone," Val protested, in answer the brothers' teasing. "In all the time since I first spoke to your Father, one of you has always been right there. I couldn't get even a private word!"

"Time enough for that after the wedding," Jamie grumbled.

"You're a fine one to talk," Ruth complained. "You were betrothed one day and married the next."

Jamie and Sophia exchanged a glance that smouldered, and Ruth wished her entire family far, far away, so she could have another of Val's kisses.

Soon enough, though, and meanwhile there were two little girls, dancing in circles holding hands, proclaiming that Lady Ruth was to be their mother. Ruth offered her hands and was taken into the circle, and then the three of them were joined by Val, all four dancing for joy in ever more dizzy circles.

One family, now and forever.

28

———

L*ondon, 1ˢᵗ December 1813*
The opening of the clinic was a huge success, despite the fog and the cold that had made this one of the most unpleasant winters on record. Val was pleased that Ruth had the crowds, and that they willingly opened their purses. In truth, he had already funded the salary of the resident doctor and the running costs for the first six months, but Ruth, tutored by her sister-in-law and cousins, was determined that the clinic had multiple sponsors. "If they pay for it, they will support it politically and socially," she told Val. "Besides"—her eyes twinkled—"if you want to spend your money supporting my work, I can think of other places that need a clinic."

Winshire had suggested opening in the Spring, in part because of the weather and in part out of safety concerns. Wharton and his chief lieutenants, including Elspeth and the Weasel, had been rescued from the convoy transporting them to London. Rumour said they had left the same day, on a ship bound for the West Indies, but Winshire feared they might have commissioned retaliation before they departed.

Ruth insisted on going ahead with the opening anyway. "The bad weather makes it all the more imperative that we are open.

We'll see more accidents, more agues, more illness and injuries of all types."

Val had hovered watchfully whenever Ruth came down to supervise the last-minute arrangements to ready the clinic, and so had her brothers and their guards, but there had been no threats. Except to Val's equanimity, since his busy betrothed had little time to be whisked into a private corner for kisses and a little more, though not nearly as much as he wished.

Coming back from the clinic opening tonight, she had looked eminently kissable, flushed with happiness and bubbling with excitement over how well the evening had gone. Val had accepted the invitation to come in for a drink, hoping for a moment with her, even if only to talk, but her sister and cousins had carried her off upstairs, insisting they all needed to rest before the journey tomorrow. Val had come home, but was too restless to sleep and was instead sitting by his window thinking about his beloved.

Tomorrow, they would leave for Shropshire and Winds' Gate. Val hoped that the old building, which purportedly sprawled over dozens of levels up and down a mountain top, had lots of private corners, and that his betrothed would be less preoccupied now that her clinic was functioning.

It would also, however, be full of his family and hers. His daughters and their nurse were already in Shropshire with Sophia and Jamie, and they would want his time and attention, especially since, in three and a half weeks, he and Ruth would be wed and leaving for their wedding journey. If he had to, he could wait until then.

He smiled at the thought, and then froze at a sound outside his window. A scrape. Another. Stealthily, he reached into his boot for his knife, forgetting that he'd taken both boots off not fifteen minutes ago.

Someone pushed at the locked window. The light of his lamp shone on the wavering glass and he couldn't see more than a shape through the distorted reflection. He narrowed his eyes as the intruder knocked on the glass, a small hand coming into focus as it rapped. Once. Twice. Wait! He recognised that hand, and the ring upon it.

He couldn't get the window open fast enough. Ruth fell into his arms as the casement swung. He managed to surface from the kiss for long enough to ask, "Beloved, what on earth are you doing here?"

"I could not sleep," Ruth told him. "And I wanted to see you, my love." That was worth another kiss, but some small part of his brain insisted on complaining.

"You did not come here alone, I hope."

Ruth pointed out the window to Val's garden, where two figures, heavily cloaked, waited patiently. "Zyba and Jeyhun escorted me." She waved and they returned the gesture, then left, letting themselves out the garden gate. "They will be back for me in an hour."

Val cupped her face with his hand. "Are you sure?" A silly thing to ask, when she had come out on a night like this and—Heaven bless him—climbed the side of his house to reach him.

"We will be married in three weeks, my dearest gentleman. We will have no time to ourselves on the journey, and very little once we get to Winds' Gate, what with the wedding preparations and Sophia about to give birth. I have been so busy, and I have missed you. I am very sure that I am precisely where I want to be."

She looked down at her feet and flushed slightly. "I do not know what I am doing, Val. But I am willing to learn."

Once—it seemed a long time ago—Val had climbed in the window of her sickroom, starting their love journey. It was only fitting that the next stage should begin with her climbing in his window. "In that case," he told her, as he led her to the bed, "come with me and I will show you."

THE END

This is the second novel in *The Return of the Mountain King*. The first, *To Wed a Proper Lady*, tells the story of Jamie Winderfield, who has been ordered to find a proper English bride, but can't persuade Sophia Belvoir, the one he has fallen in love with, that he is serious about her.

The next novel in the series is *To Claim the Long-Lost Lover*, which will be out in June or July. But before then comes *Melting Matilda*, a novella telling of the courtship of the Duchess of Haverford's ward.

Read on for **more about the Mountain King series**.

ENJOY THESE BOOKS BY JUDE KNIGHT

Regency books

The Return of the Mountain King series

James Winderfield, exiled third son of the Duke of Winshire, is back to inherit the ducal title.

In 1812, high Society is rocked by the return of the Earl of Sutton, heir to the dying Duke of Winshire. James Winderfield, Earl of Sutton, Winshire's third and only surviving son, has long been thought dead, but his reappearance is not nearly such a shock as those he brings with him, the children of his deceased Persian-born wife and fierce armed retainers, both men and women.

The Duke of Haverford, his one-time rival in love, sets out to destroy him, and his children with him, but Sutton is no longer the friendless, open-hearted youth that was exiled for his temerity. Even inheriting his father's title won't stop his enemies from trying to kill him. But no one, his people whisper, ever wins against the King of the Mountains.

As the new Duke of Winshire's four older children and his twin nieces navigate society to find acceptance and a love of their own, Winshire rekindles his acquaintance with the influential and beloved matriarch, Eleanor, Duchess of Haverford. Their time is long past; their friendship, though, is golden.

Paradise Regained (prequel novella)

James yearns to end a long journey in the arms of his loving family. But his father's agents offer the exiled prodigal forgiveness and a place in Society — if he abandons his foreign-born wife and children to return to England.

With her husband away, Mahzad faces revolt, invasion and betrayal in the mountain kingdom they built together. A queen without her king, she will not allow their dream and their family to be destroyed.

To Wed a Proper Lady — The Barbarian and the Bluestocking (novel 1 in the series)

Everyone knows James needs a bride with impeccable blood lines. He needs Sophia's love more.

James, eldest son of the Earl of Sutton, must marry to please his grandfather, the Duke of Winshire, and to win social acceptance for himself and his father's other foreign-born children. But only Lady Sophia Belvoir makes his heart sing, and to win her, he must invite himself to spend Christmas at the home of his father's greatest enemy: the man who is fighting in Parliament to have his father's marriage declared invalid and the Winderfield children made bastards.

Sophia keeps secret her *tendre* for James, Lord Elfingham. After all, the whole of Society knows he is pursuing the younger Belvoir sister, not the older one left on the shelf after two failed betrothals. Even when he asks for her hand in marriage, she still can't quite believe that he loves her.

(This book was first published as a novella, and has been extensively rewritten to make it a novel. The novella was in the Bluestocking Belles' collection *Holly and Hopeful Hearts*.)

A Suitable Husband

A chef from the slums, however talented, is no fit mate for the cousin of a duke, however distant. But Cedrica Grenford can dream. (novella)

To Mend the Broken-Hearted — The Healer and the Hermit (This book: Novel 2)

Trained as a healer, Ruth Winderfield is happiest in a sickroom. When she's caught up in a smallpox epidemic and finds herself quarantined at the remote manor of a reclusive lord, the last thing she expects is to find her heart's desire. A pity he does not feel the same. She must return to London's ballrooms, where the wealth of her family and the question over her birth make her a target for the unscrupulous and a pariah to the high-sticklers.

Valentine, Earl of Ashbury, is horrified when an impertinent bossy female turns up with several sick children, including the two girls he is responsible for. He hasn't seen his niece and his daughter—if she is his daughter—since his faithless wife and treacherous brother died three years ago. He reluctantly gives them shelter. Even more reluctantly, he helps with the nursing.

When Ruth goes, she takes his heart with him. When jealous relatives lie about their time together, Val must face his past and win her back, not just for himself, but for the children he has come to love.

Melting Matilda (A novella in the Bluestocking Belle's collection, Fire & Frost, published as stand-alone in May 2021)

Sparks flew a year ago when the Granite Earl kissed the Ice Princess under the mistletoe. Matilda Grenford is a lady and the ward of a duchess, but the daughter of a famous courtesan. Charles, Earl of Hamner, seeks a countess of impeccable bloodlines, not one whose scandalous birth would offend every noble ancestor back to the Norman Conquest. But neither of them can forget that kiss.

Coming at two-monthly intervals from July 2021

To Tame the Wild Rake — The Sinner and the Saint

The Marquis of Aldridge doesn't want to yearn for the sister of a friend from his raking days. Especially since she has rejected him in no uncertain terms. Charlotte Winderfield, niece of the Mountain King, keeps a secret that bars her from marriage, but even if she found the courage to trust, she would never trust a rake.

To Claim the Long-Lost Lover — The Diamond and the Doctor

Her girlhood lover is back, as compelling as ever, but Sarah Winderfield, Charlotte's twin, cannot forget he abandoned her, leaving her to face the anger of her family and worse. Sarah is even lovelier than when she was a girl, but Miles Pointon has not forgiven her for betraying him to her father's revenge: indenture to the Caribbean and years of servitude.

The Golden Redepennings series

True love is rare and elusive, but they won't settle for less.

Candle's Christmas Chair (A novella in *The Golden Redepennings* series)

They are separated by social standing and malicious lies. He has until Christmas to convince her to give their love another chance.

Gingerbread Bride (A novella in *The Golden Redepennings* series)

Mary runs from an unwanted marriage and finds adventure, danger and her girlhood hero, coming once more to her rescue.

Farewell to Kindness (Book 1 in *The Golden Redepennings* series)

Love is not always convenient. Anne and Rede have different goals, but when their enemies join forces, so must they.

A Raging Madness (Book 2 in *The Golden Redepennings* series)

Their marriage is a fiction. Their enemies are all too real. Uncovering the truth will need all the trust Ella and Alex can find.

<u>*The Realm of Silence*</u> (Book 3 in *The Golden Redepennings* series)

Rescue her daughter, destroy her dragons, defeat his demons, return to his lonely life. How hard can it be?

<u>*Unkept Promises*</u> (Book 4 in *The Golden Redepennings* series)

Mia hopes to negotiate a comfortable marriage. Jules wants his wife to return to England, where she belongs. Love confounds them both.

Other Regency books

<u>*A Baron for Becky*</u>

She was a fallen woman. How could the men who loved her help set her back on her feet?

<u>*House of Thorns*</u>

His rose thief bride comes with a scandal that threatens to tear them apart.

<u>*Lord Calne's Christmas Ruby*</u>

One wealthy merchant's heiress with an aversion to fortune hunters. One an impoverished earl with a twisted hand. Combine and stir with one villainous rector. (novella)

<u>*Revealed in Mist*</u>

As spy and enquiry agent, Prue and David worked to uncover secrets, while hiding a few of their own.

The Beast Next Door (A novella in the Bluestocking Belles collection *Valentines from Bath)*

In all the assemblies and parties, no-one Charis met could ever match the beast next door.

Lunch-length reads: story collections

Hand-Turned Tales and *Lost in the Tale*

A double handful of short stories and novellas. *Hand-Turned Tales* is free from most eretailers. Try the range of Jude's imagination one bite at a time, in a lunch-length read.

If Mistletoe Could Tell Tales

A repackaging of six published Christmas stories: four novellas and two novelettes. Because nothing enhances the magic of Christmas like the magic of love.

Hearts in the Land of Ferns

Five stories all set in New Zealand: two historical and three contemporary suspense. All That Glisters has been published in Hand-Turned Tales. The other four have all been published in multi-author collections, but never before in a collection of Jude Knight stories.

ABOUT JUDE KNIGHT

I've been trying to be a novelist since I was fourteen. I was a good enough reader to see that the first two attempts (one when I was fourteen and one in my early twenties) weren't good enough to publish. Then along came life. A seriously ill child who required years of therapy; a rising mortgage that led to a full-time job; my own chronic illness… the writing took a back seat.

As the years passed, the fear grew. I'd waited so long. If I never finished any of the dozens of novels I started, no one would ever judge them.

My mother believed in me, and on the way home from that great lady's funeral, I realised I'd left it too late for Mum to ever hold a print copy of one of my fiction books. So I replaced the fear of finishing with the fear of not finishing, by telling everyone I knew that I was writing a novel.

In the years since I published my first fiction book just before Christmas in 2014, I published seven novels, thirteen novellas, a heap of shorter stories, and more novellas in group anthologies. I plan to keep going till I run out of years.

I write historical fiction with a large helping of romance, a splash of Regency, and a twist of suspense.

I then try to figure out how to slot it into a genre category.

I'm mad keen on history, enjoy what happens to people in the crucible of a passionate relationship, and love to use a good mystery and some real danger as mechanisms to torture my characters.

In my other identity as Judy Knighton, I've been a plain language consultant specialising in contracts, insurance policies, and financial disclosure statements. Fiction is more fun.

Website and blog: http://judeknightauthor.com/
Book blurbs and links: http://judeknightauthor.com/books/

Do you like news before anyone else, plus discounts, and free stuff?

Sign up to my newsletter. The main newsletter goes out once every two months, and includes news about coming books, discounts, contests, and events. Every newsletter also has news about books from my author friends, and a free story that I write just for newsletter subscribers.

In between newsletters, if I have something exciting to share I occasionally sends a one-topic email.

Free book as a thank you

As a thank you for subscribing to my newsletter, you can expect a series of three emails, the first offering a free copy of one of my books, and the next two with links to other free stories. So why not subscribe today?

Subscribe to newsletter: http://judeknightauthor.com/newsletter/

www.ingramcontent.com/pod-product-compliance
Lightning Source LLC
Chambersburg PA
CBHW021657110726
47902CB00007B/1969